# THE END OF DARKNESS

**by**

**Jaime Rush**

Cover image by Linnea Sinclair
Photograph of Scott Nova by Ken Tilley
Fotoimages by Ken



Discover other paranormal romance titles by Jaime Rush at www.JaimeRush.com and romantic suspense novels by Tina Wainscott at www.TinaWainscott.com.

What others are saying about
THE END OF DARKNESS

*The End of Darkness* was everything I needed to complete the *Offspring* series. It was action packed, intense, passionate and included a subplot involving my favorite emotionally challenged Callorian. Yes, the ending was bittersweet; it made me cry, but it was a good cry. – Mel Thomas, Smashattackreads.com

Longtime fans of Rush's Offspring series will be pleased to learn that Rush is self-publishing the thrilling conclusion to her suspenseful series that featured intriguing elements of the paranormal and extraterrestrial. This finale addresses not only the romantic relationship of Magnus McLeod, but also Pope, the mysterious alien featured throughout the series. Kudos to Rush for creating and delivering an exceptional romantic suspense series! –Jill M. Smith, RT Bookreviews

The End of Darkness is fast-paced, emotional and hot!
–Sulia

What others are saying about
THE OFFSPRING SERIES

If you enjoy Paranormal Romance with a great deal of action, this is definitely the series for you. ~ Larissa's Bookish Life http://www.larissaslife.com/

If you are looking for a new addiction, then look no further than Jaime Rush's compelling series, THE OFFSPRING. ~ Romance Junkies

Jaime's OFFSPRING series is AMAZEBALLS!!!! I've been a fan since the very first book A Perfect Darkness came out in 2009 and I've been hooked ever since. If you have not read this series yet, you are SO missing out!! ~ Carla Gallway, Book Monster Reviews

# DEDICATION

This book, and the whole Offspring series, is dedicated to my fans. Thank you for your book-love. I have treasured every email and correspondence, every post and review, and your friendship.

Thanks especially to my Rushkies, my street team! You all have gone above and beyond, and for that I'm so very grateful.

Thanks to the blog mistresses and misters who have featured my books. Your dedication to sharing your love of books is phenomenal!

To Marisa Cleveland and Nicole Resciniti for your input on the book and for being wonderful all on your own.

To Tammy Walp for your help in the final stages of production.

And to Stephen Borden. I'm proud of you for getting through a tough time and coming out on top, smile intact.

# THE END OF DARKNESS

**By**

**Jaime Rush**

# CHAPTER 1

Magnus McLeod came to with a violent start, sitting up so fast, the room spun. Even so, he instantly knew this wasn't his bedroom. Or a hospital. Lachlan stood next to his bed with an odd expression, both relieved and like he was about to tell Magnus his legs were missing.

Lachlan leaned forward and held him tight for a few moments. "Thank God."

Magnus hardly enjoyed the hug, preoccupied with wanting to make sure his body parts were intact. The second Lachlan stepped back, Magnus did a visual check. Legs, aye, and they moved at his command. Arms, fingers, all accounted for.

Lachlan peered into Magnus's face. "You alright, Maggie?" The childhood nickname Lachlan had given him when Magnus started calling him Locky, a bit of teasing between two brothers.

"Seem to be, other than feeling muzzy, like I was on a bender and slept for twenty-four hours." He rubbed his hand over his face, feeling several days' worth of beard. "How long *have* I been sleeping? Where am I? What happened?" He took in the room with its light brown walls and framed pictures of the Wizard of Oz.

Lachlan said, "You're in Cheveyo and Petra's guest room in downtown Annapolis. They've been taking care of you while Jessie and I dealt with her uncle. Which felt like it lasted for weeks but was only a few days."

"Jessie." Magnus pictured the lass he was keen on, a pixie of a thing with brown hair. "I've been stuck in this dream about being at the carnival and some man trying to hurt her. I tried to protect her, and he turned into a black beast." His hand went to his neck, but the words cut as deeply as the memory of claws slicing his throat.

Bloody hell. *Memory*, not a dream.

"You were killed," Lachlan said softly.

"Jessie?" He looked beyond Lachlan, finding no one else in the room. Cold fear washed over him. "Is she alright?"

"Aye, she's fine now." Lachlan shook his head. "That's the kind of guy you are. I tell you that you died, and you're worried about her."

"You say it like it's a bad thing."

Lachlan's laugh had no humor. "No, it just shows what a damned good guy you are."

Again, sounded like a bad thing.

Lachlan leaned against the side of the bed. "She healed you."

"Healed psychically?" He felt a thrumming energy in his body, an odd heaviness as though his soul had gained a hundred pounds. Which made no sense.

Lachlan's expression darkened. "You were dying, just like I saw in the vision I warned you about."

Aye, the vision where Lachlan had seen Magnus dead at the carnival, Jessie standing over him. "You did see the future. I guess you'll toss me an 'I told you so' and deservedly so. Who was the guy that tried to kill me?"

Lachlan leaned against the footboard. "Her uncle. Bastard was hunting her for years. He's dead now," he added when Magnus stiffened at the thought of the guy hurting her. "What happened in the days after your attack, why Jessie was on the run, that's a story for later."

"He turned into a bloody beast. That wasn't my imagination, right? Because over and over I've been living it, seeing him morph into a black creature."

"It wasn't your imagination." Lachlan released a long breath. "You need to understand that you were dying, and we had to make a choice. Jessie and I."

The mention of her name had Magnus glancing at the door. "Where is she? I need to see her."

"You were right when you told me there was something special about her. She's got enhanced abilities like us, but she's not an Offspring."

Magnus digested that for a moment. "So that means what, that she didn't have a parent in the same secret government program Dad was in?" The program for psychically gifted people who were given the DNA of a bloke from a parallel dimension to enhance their abilities—DNA their offspring inherited.

"Her father is *from* the other dimension. And she was even more special. She held Darkness. So did the man who turned to beast. In the parallel dimension, they aren't allowed to express their emotions, so they repress them. All those emotions accumulated into this mass of energy called Darkness. Jessie's father and uncle tapped into it and drew it into their bodies. They could channel it to change into an animal of sorts. As you saw."

"I saw, all right. But why are you still looking at me like I've lost a limb?"

Lachlan's jaw tensed. "The price of Jessie's healing was that she had to infuse Darkness into you. I told her to do it. I made the choice."

Something inside Magnus went numb as Lachlan's words sank in. "So that…beast is in me?" That had to be the heaviness he felt.

"You can choose what form it takes by focusing on a particular animal. Jessie's dad will work with you. You have to learn to control Darkness, or it'll take you over."

"Bloody great."

Magnus pulled himself to the side of the bed and tested his weight. His legs were shaky. Lachlan moved closer, hands out to steady him. Magnus used the headboard to stand. "Where is Jessie?" At Lachlan's ever-darkening expression, his chest tightened. "I need to see her." That need raged through him, making him want to start tearing furniture apart until someone brought her to him.

Lachlan drove his fingers back through hair much shorter and neater than Magnus had ever seen it. "You can't. Darkness has other side effects. It can make you volatile when you experience high emotions. And it makes you possessive and madly jealous to the point of being deadly to anyone you see as a rival to the woman you feel is yours."

"I don't feel she's mine." They hadn't even kissed, but he did feel…oddly possessive, aye. "It's just that

I've spent days of unconsciousness caught in a loop of those last several minutes with her."

Lachlan shifted from one foot to the other. "She's at Sanctuary." Their family compound in the woods.

Magnus knew that nervous shift. He'd seen it whenever Lachlan was about to admit he'd broken something, like the time he'd put a ding on Magnus's sword when they were lads. "Out with it, Locky. What aren't you telling me?"

Lachlan bowed his head, pain wracking his features. No, this was worse than anything like that. "I'm the lowest of the low. She and I went through hell together. We fought the pull between us, I swear it. I tried to be an arse—as you know I can be—but she saw something inside me even I didn't see." He met Magnus's gaze. "I love her. I didn't mean to, but I love her, and all I can do is ask your forgiveness."

He knew his brother would never do anything to hurt him, and his regret was clear. So was his love for Jessie. So why did the words, "*You stole my girl while I was recuperating*?" come roaring out of his mouth?

Lachlan hung his head. "She wasn't your girl yet, but aye, that's the bottom line. I am pond scum. The scum that lives beneath the pond scum."

Anger unfurled inside him. Even weak, Magnus was big enough to pound Lachlan but good. He took a deep breath, pulling back all that fury, and made his way to the window to stare out into an alley between the townhouses. "I forgive you." He meant it, but the words still felt gritty as they left his mouth. "You're right, she wasn't my girl." He turned to Lachlan from a safer distance. "So this Darkness is why I want to smash in your head over it?"

Lachlan's mouth tightened. "Aye. I deserve it, too, but I'd rather you not. I don't want to lose you over it, but I could no sooner break it off with her than cut off my hand. Once you've met someone else, you'll move on. Remember what you told me not long ago: the feelings you have for a woman always fizzle out like a soda left out too long."

Aye, he had said that, and he'd experienced it many a time. But Jessie felt different. Now he knew why.

Lachlan waved his hand dismissively. "You'll find other women. Hell, you draw them like flies."

Magnus crossed his arms over his chest. "Thanks for that lovely analogy. Makes me sound like a pile of shite."

"I was thinking a candy bar or maybe a glob of jelly on the sidewalk."

It felt like one of many exchanges, but everything was different now. Lachlan was happy and in love, both new for him. Magnus held something otherworldly and dangerous.

He didn't want another woman. He breathed Jessie, the need for her. The need to posses her. He felt her in his cells, something he'd never experienced before. Nor had he ever felt jealousy. If a woman he was dating wanted to move on, Magnus wished her well with nary a hard feeling. He flexed his fingers. "And if I feel proprietary about a woman, I'll hurt anyone who flirts with her? Or hurt the woman?" An unfathomable thought.

"Potentially. I'm sorry for what comes with Darkness, but not for making the decision. I wasn't going to let you die."

No, he wouldn't, not after everything they'd already lost. "I would have done the same, brother." The sight of his sword, leaning against the wall with the tip buried in the carpet, brought comfort. He picked it up, running his fingers down the flat part of the blade. "You took a chance bringing this here."

"It's like an old friend. Thought you might like it nearby."

Magnus swung it around, holding the blade a foot away from Lachlan. "Were you not afraid I'd cleave off your head when I found out about Jessie?"

Lachlan remained still, no fear on his face. "You've got a much deadlier weapon inside you now. If you're of a mind to kill me, I'm going one way or another."

Magnus held the sword up, studying the ornate hilt. He wouldn't need his sword anymore? How much more would he lose?

A knock sounded on the door, and Cheveyo opened it and peered inside. "Everything all right?" His Hopi heritage was clear in his coloring and dark hair. That he'd once spent his days hunting down supernatural vermin showed in his warrior bearing. Especially when he saw the sword in Magnus's hand and stepped inside, ready to contain him.

Magnus let him know that wouldn't be necessary by setting the sword down. He reached over and shook Cheveyo's hand. "Thanks for everything."

He'd only met Cheveyo once, Petra a few more times, so it was damned nice of them to take care of him. Made him feel odd though, being passed out at their house.

"You'll be okay," Cheveyo said. "I don't know how similar Darkness is to my ability, but when I get worked up, my cat wants to take over. You need to practice, get comfortable with Darkness, because control is everything. I have a place out near Flagstaff, Arizona. Why don't you spend some time in new surroundings?" Away from Jessie, he didn't say. "Take as long as you want. We're staying here, waiting for Amy to have her baby. I couldn't pry Petra away now. Stay for the shower and then head out."

Magnus had planned on attending the baby shower, since the guys in their group of Offspring were invited too. That was before he'd been infected. The heavy feeling was like the blackest part of the night inside him. "I'm not in the mood for the party, but I have gifts for the baby." He pinned Lachlan with a look. "You'll take them, right?" Make him go to a baby shower, small retribution for stealing his lass.

"Anything for you," Lachlan said, clearly meaning it. But Magnus saw his upper lip twitch at the thought.

Anything but give up Jessie.

He turned to Cheveyo. "Your place sounds like exactly what I need." Especially if Lachlan and Jessie were staying at Sanctuary.

Lachlan walked closer. "Spend some time with Jessie's dad. He'll tell you what you need to know." He put his hand on Magnus's arm. "Take a week or so, work through it. But keep in touch. My brother once told me that we had to stick together because we were all we have."

But that was before one of them became a beast…and the other fell in love.

Erica Evrard trolled through her Google Alerts, just like she did every night. Only the computer screen lit up the small bedroom, splashing pale light over a desk covered in notes and maps, and a bed she shared with no one.

First post: a new serial killer novel coming out from Erica Fleming. Not a well-known author, just a woman trying to make a small living from writing novels based on the wretchedness she read about in all those newspaper stories. The evil she faced down in dark places. She deleted that one.

The second entry detailed a possible serial killer in Strasford, Arizona, a sick son of a bitch who ripped out people's hearts while they were still alive. The authorities were baffled, not completely ruling out a wild animal, given the claw marks left behind. That the bodies were left intact made it seem more like a sick human act. The three victims were female visitors to the small desert town not far from Las Vegas.

The serial killer wasn't the locals' only concern. They'd been experiencing tremors, despite the fact that no fault line existed beneath their town. People were on edge, prone to violent attacks and fits of rage. A seismologist was investigating the tremors, but they had no leads as far as the so-called Heart Ripper was concerned.

She stared at the lines that crisscrossed the backs of her hands and arms. Every time she used the ability she'd dubbed Lightning, because of how the lines looked, the scars moved farther up her arms. Closer to her heart.

She mapped the route to Strasford and shut down her computer. Time to pack and hunt down a killer.

# CHAPTER 2

**O**ne week later…

Erica stepped out of the chilly night and into a loud, warm bar. Places like this—rough around the edges, smelling of beer and smoke—seemed like a second home. Killers and rapists often hung out in them to troll for their next victim and sometimes to brag. She was good at putting out the victim vibe because she'd been one. Finally she'd figured out that body language attracted abusive men. Now she could spot the vibe in others: the hunched shoulders and downcast eyes, the way a woman carried herself as though she expected abuse. Deserved it. No woman deserved to be treated with anything but respect. Erica put on the act when *she* trolled for a killer.

Not that she'd found him yet. But this was her hunting ground. Two of the victims had come in here. Erica headed toward an empty stool at the bar. The band on the small stage was banging out a not-half-bad version of *Born to be Wild*.

Speaking of not half bad…as she took one of the stools, her gaze lit on the drummer. Even though he was in back, he was eye-catching: big and muscular, wearing a tank top that showcased his enormous biceps. He tossed a head of curls as he gave himself to the music, his eyes closed, mouth curved in a smile. His passion intoxicated her.

*No time for that.*

That's what her mind said. Another part of her, one she never dared look at too closely, said otherwise. It unfurled a need inside her that tightened her chest. *You know how well that works out. Sex that feels good for, oh, about three minutes. Then that awful sense of shame and dissatisfaction.*

"Miss?"

She turned to the bartender, who'd set a napkin in front of her. "Killian's, please." She liked the red beers, though she always nursed the one all night. When he set the bottle in front of her, she said, "The band's great."

The man beamed. "Thanks. That's my son, playing bass."

She took in the gangly young man on guitar, but her gaze slid right past him to the drummer again. "He's good. So is the drummer."

"Yeah, he is. Magnus, I think his name is. Something Scottish. A godsend he was. The band's drummer got into a fist fight right before the first set." He shook his head. "Both hotheads went to the hospital with broken noses. That guy stepped up and said he could use the sticks. And he's right."

So he likely wasn't a local. Could he be her killer? Anticipation tightened her chest. She watched Magnus through the next four songs, playing as cohesively as if he'd been with the band for years. In between, she chatted up the bartender. "Someone mentioned that tempers have been flaring a lot around here lately.

Yesterday a woman threw the gas nozzle because it wouldn't pump. Earlier that day, a man nearly punched a cashier, because the register didn't ring up the sale price."

The man's expression turned grim. "I think the tremors have everyone on edge. We've never had them before so we're not used to thinking in terms of earthquakes."

"Having a serial killer in the area probably isn't helping."

"I think it's an animal, but either way it's not great for attracting tourists."

When the band finally took a break, Magnus and the others made a beeline for the end of the bar. The bartender served them a pitcher of beer. Magnus ordered a Guinness, asserting that American beers tasted like piss-water. They launched into a deep discussion on the qualities of beer and why drinking it cold made it even worse (Magnus's opinion, in stark contrast to the other guys'). Magnus's eyes crinkled when he smiled, and he had a low, infectious laugh.

He slung back the rest of his mug and headed toward the back of the bar. He had to pass her on his way, and she watched to see if he was searching the crowd for a potential victim. His gaze remained ahead, maybe where the restrooms were. But as he passed, he turned to her. She felt a frisson of electricity like a mild shock when his brown eyes met hers.

She spoke before he could continue. "You're good. I mean, on the drums."

"Thanks. I'm just filling in. I was in a band back in Maryland."

She'd have to see if there'd been any murders in Maryland recently. She held out her hand. "I'm Erica."

"I'm called Magnus."

Their hands connected, and she felt the frisson even more. He seemed to feel it, too, because he looked down at their clasped hands.

"Where are you from?" he asked.

She was from Maryland too, originally, but that time of her life brought back too many painful memories. "Kansas City, Missouri." A lonely apartment she was rarely at.

He released her hand slowly and nodded toward the back. "I have to hit the loo before our next set." He arched a thick eyebrow. "Any requests?"

She was startled by the one that popped into her mind: *Take Another Little Piece of My Heart*. "I Can't Get No Satisfaction," she said instead. That fit her sex life.

"I think I can fix you right up." He gave her a smile she was sure had 'fixed up' many a woman. Especially along with his slight Scottish accent. Was he flirting?

The thought tickled her stomach as she watched him weave around the tables, pausing to collect another compliment on his drumming before disappearing down the hallway. Had he meant he could fix her up *that* way? She wasn't good at flirting, so she knew nothing of the subtleties. Most of the men she had sex with didn't either. In bars like this, it was more like, "Wanna go someplace else?"

Magnus gave her another smile as he passed by on the way to the stage, where the band prepared for the next set. He had a certain grace to his gait despite his size. All muscle, strong enough to…well, to rip out a woman's heart?

*Don't get caught up in that boyish charm. Ted Bundy was boyish, too.*

Their gazes met throughout the set, which included *Can't Get No Satisfaction* and, coincidentally, *Take Another Little Piece of My Heart*. Janis had a tragically short life, a concept that spoke to Erica's soul.

At two in the morning, the band finished their final set to the applause of those who were left. Erica leaned against the bar, facing the stage, blatantly watching Magnus. His gaze went to hers as she clapped, too. He made his way over, rubbing a towel across the back of his neck. If he were the killer, then she could end this now and go back to her little apartment. If he wasn't, she could…

*Hope to find what you haven't in all those other encounters?* her snotty inner voice piped in.

The thing she craved, probably because she could never have it. Love. Normalcy.

*Yeah, take another piece of my heart.*

She enjoyed the spark between them as he sat down beside her. It wasn't something she often felt. "Thanks for playing my song," she said. "How did you know the Janis Joplin one was my favorite?" She tried to give him a playful smile, but the coincidence was eerie.

He dipped his chin a little, all serious-like. "Maybe I'm psychic."

*Whoa*. This guy was pushing all the right buttons.

He tilted his head back, closed his eyes, and said, "Let me see what else I can pick up. You're from out of town. You're here for..." His eyes opened. "A dark reason." He wasn't altogether kidding.

She forced a laugh, freaked by how on target he was. "Setting research. I write suspense novels about killers."

"Ah, that explains it. Any romance in these books?"

Not usually. She had no idea what romance was. "There's sex in them."

Maybe he'd ask if she needed research help with that aspect. She hoped he wasn't a killer, because something about him...

"Hey, Magnus, we're heading back to Chip's place. You want to go?"

Magnus was leaving. That thought tightened her throat. She expected him to bid her goodnight.

"Do I want to go?" he asked her instead.

"Stay," she heard herself say.

"I'm good, thanks. See you tomorrow night, if you need me. You have my number." He waved at them and turned to her. "We could go somewhere quiet."

She slid from her stool. "Your place?" If she thought a guy was a potential killer, she wanted to go back to his place. That way she didn't have a body to deal with in her own motel room. Although Lightning made it look like they'd died from a heart attack, she didn't want to have to answer any awkward questions.

"My place is about an hour from here. I drove out this morning, just exploring. The guys in the band were going to let me crash at their place for the night so I didn't have to drive back so late."

He'd lost his place to stay because of her. She assessed him. Unlike psychopaths, Magnus's eyes were deep and rich. Not flat and emotionless. She saw not a killer gleam but a hint of the same hunger she felt.

Bryan Adams's old song, *Lonely Nights*, played in her mind:

*Baby, I just can't stand another lonely night,*

*So come over and save me…*

And more importantly, he probably wouldn't make her disappear when the band and bartender could place him with her.

"Then let's go back to my motel room," she said.

He followed in a black BMW, taking turns way too fast. Anticipation and trepidation fluttered in her stomach. She felt something with Magnus she'd never felt. That electricity between them. *Remember who you are. Why you're here.*

How could she forget? She looked at the long sleeves of her shirt, imagining the scars beneath them and what they meant. She'd never had the experience of falling in love for the first time, losing her virginity to a man of her choice. Sexuality had always been wrapped in shame and anger.

Once inside the room, Magnus said, "I'd like to shower up, if that's all right. A night playing in a bar leaves me grotty." He gave her a playful look. "Want to join me?"

The question took her off guard, the thought of exposing herself like that… "No. Go ahead though."

He took a quick shower, stepping out of the bathroom with a towel wrapped around his waist. He had a beautiful body, tanned, not a scar on him…and an erection that showed through the thin terry cloth. The sight of it stirred that primal part of her.

He must have sensed it because his eyes flared with the same kind of lust. He walked closer, smelling of soap, and pulled her close. His mouth came down on hers, gentle despite his ardor. She didn't like kissing, but he eased her in, nudging her lips apart and tempting her into opening to him.

This was the part of the one-night stand where she didn't feel so damned lonely. When, for the next hour or so, she wasn't alone. This part was okay. She could fool herself that it would be different this time. That she would feel something.

And it was. Magnus kissed her, taking his time rather than pushing her right down on the bed and getting down to business. Which would be great if she weren't messed up. His hands cupped her face, thumbs stroking her jaw, his kisses growing more intense. He eased her out of her shirt, kissing her neck and shoulders with a tenderness that made her want to cry. She wasn't used to this. He unhooked her bra and started to pull it away. Yeah, he knew what he was doing.

"Wait," she whispered, holding her bra to her breasts and backing up toward the door. She hit the light switch, plunging them into darkness.

"Why'd you do that? I can't see a bloody thing. And I want to see you."

"I don't feel comfortable with the lights on."

Silence as he perhaps pondered that. "Is it some kind of hang up? I can help you get over that. Because what I saw was beautiful."

He might even mean it. He sounded sincere, anyway. She moved back into his embrace, letting her bra fall away. "I don't want to get over it. I just want it dark." She unzipped her pants and shoved both them and her panties to the floor, then groped for his hand and pulled him down to the bed.

"Are you self-conscious—"

"It's not that." The words had come out tersely.

He started to back away. "If you're uncomfortable—"

"No." She reached out, feeling the expanse of his chest, and then went lower and wrapped her fingers around his penis. "I'm very comfortable. In the dark. Please humor me." She didn't usually say 'please.' Usually she let them leave if they balked.

He released a breath, but she couldn't tell whether it was out of frustration or in reaction to her hand on him. Either way, he relented, lying down beside her. She kissed him, wanting to feel his mouth on hers again. He ran his hands down her body, over her stomach, nestling in her pubic hair. His fingers rubbed provocatively back and forth as he moved from her mouth to her jaw and down her neck.

Desire swirled through her, different from anything she'd ever felt. She felt the urge to let go, to flow down that lazy river. But letting go meant losing control, so she pulled herself back.

"You alright?" he asked, running the words together.

Had she stiffened? He was eerily perceptive. "Fine. Wonderful. But you don't have to do all this…kissing and touching. I know guys want to get to it. I'm fine with that."

She thought he lifted his head because she no longer felt his mouth on her collarbone.

"Erica, I don't know what kind of blokes you've been with, but I like to take my time. And I like to make sure the woman I'm with gets as much out of it as I do. I want to hear you screaming and panting before I'm done."

Those words shivered through her. Except screaming would mean losing control, something she never, ever did.

"No, please, just…shag me. I want you so much I can't wait for anything else." She wondered if he could hear the lie in her breathless words.

"You don't want me to go down on you?" He sounded baffled. "Women tell me that's the only way they can come. And there's nothing like the sound a woman makes when my tongue—"

"No, I don't want that."

"You're sure you want any of this? I mean, I'm up for it, but you seem conflicted."

"I do want this, and I'm not conflicted." She did want it. Her body ached for it, and something else, something deeper. Why was he questioning her? He was getting easy sex. Isn't that what most men wanted? "I want you, Magnus. I want you inside me. Now."

She pushed him flat on the bed, then climbed on top of him. She took him in hand and fumbled with the drawer where she'd thrown a condom. Even though she'd promised herself she wouldn't do this again.

He was no doubt the biggest guy she'd ever been with. Blindly, she smoothed the condom down over him. Easing in took longer than usual, stretching her, but he filled her in a way she'd never felt before. His hands came up to her waist as he guided her motions. But he wasn't trying to speed her up. No, he was taking his time. She set a fast pace, expecting him to finish in a minute or two. Then he could leave, and she could torment herself for giving in again. This was something her body wanted, but her soul always resisted.

Instead, Magnus rolled her onto her back and kissed her. She started to move her head away. She didn't like kissing, but something inside her responded to his mouth on hers, coaxing her to open to him. She did, and his tongue traced lazy circles around hers. Before she could think about it, she was matching his movements, joining the kiss.

"Can we turn on the light now?" he said between kisses.

"No. I like the dark."

His hand skimmed down her arm. "If it's the scars you're worried about, I don't care. You feel beautiful."

She squeezed her eyes shut at those words. Was this guy for real? She could only shake her head, afraid her voice would give away how that made her feel.

"Next time," he whispered against her cheek. He caressed her breast and then rubbed his thumb over her nipple. "Next time I will see you."

She shivered at the declaration, unable to tell him that there wouldn't be another time. There was never more than one encounter.

He positioned her legs on either side of his waist, gripping her hips and entering her again. The angle allowed him to drive into the deepest part of her, sending crazy sensations shooting through her. He drew one hand to her nub, where he stroked as he thrust. She had never had an orgasm, but she felt *something* as they moved together. Pressure building inside her, a throbbing where he touched her. She had never been with anyone like Magnus, a man who wanted her to experience pleasure. Who insisted on it.

He took his time, varying the rhythm. Several minutes had gone by, ten, maybe twenty. She'd lost track of time, forgetting to hope this finished fast. Hearing his breathing come in shallow pants, his low groan of pleasure, stirred her. Her breaths were coming faster, too, and her body was moving of its own volition, shifting for a better angle, speeding the pace.

*Losing control. Enjoying him too much.*

Mentally she pulled back.

His body jerked, his grip tightened, and she felt him throb inside her. He called out, "Jessie!"

Now she physically pulled away, stumbling off the bed.

"I'm sorry," he said. "I didn't mean to—"

"Call me by another woman's name." She gained her footing. "Look, it's no big deal. We hardly know each other." But she heard the anger and hurt in her voice, which didn't make any sense because they did hardly know each other.

With a *click*, the light snapped on, filling the room with glaring light. He wasn't going to hide from his blunder. In fact, he met her gaze head on. "It's not what you think."

She snatched up the sheet and covered herself. "Sounded to me like you were thinking about another woman."

He looked thrown off, shaking his head. "It wasn't like that." He went into the bathroom while she pulled on her clothes.

When he came out, she asked, "Who's Jessie?" The question came out in that terse voice again.

"She's my brother's girl."

"You were imagining your *brother's girl* while you were doing me?" The words fairly screamed out of her mouth. "That's despicable on two levels."

He rubbed his hand over his face. "I wanted the lights on. I wanted to see *you*, but you've obviously got some kind of hang up." He shook his head, pulling on his jeans and then grabbing his shirt and shrugging into it. "For some reason, coming threw me into this nightmare I've been having every night. I…" He looked as though he were in agony. "I can't explain it without sounding crazy."

"So you'd rather me think you an asshole than crazy?"

He blinked at her harsh words. "It's probably better that way. You're right, I'm an arsehole. I was hoping being with you would drive Jessie out of my cells because I felt a similar *something* with you that I did with her."

*Felt what?* she wanted to ask but held the question back. "So you were using me to purge some girl out of your system?"

"Like you were using me to get release. At least that's all I thought you wanted. Then you let down all your walls for a few minutes, and I realized you need more than that."

"I do not! Please leave now."

He met her eyes, his filled with a pain she didn't understand. "It's better this way, you despising me. I'm messed up beyond what you could ever understand."

He left, not slamming the door as she'd expect but closing it softly behind him.

Beyond what she could understand? Holy hell, he *was* the killer.

*He's a psychic killer.* Because she swore he could read her mind. The Janis Joplin song, what her soul needed that her mind refused to acknowledge, all too eerie.

Okay, maybe that was going too far. Right now she was only concerned about one thing: finding proof that he was the Heart Ripper and killing him. Erica stepped out of her room the moment his headlights slashed across her door. She was going to follow him.

# CHAPTER 3

The beast clawed at him. Magnus felt the slice across his throat, the warm blood pouring down his skin and the pain. He saw Jessie's horror-struck expression as he fell to the ground. *Can't help her. She'll die*.

"Jessie!"

He woke as he did every morning, that one word filled with his terror at the fact that he couldn't help her. He bowed his head, scrubbing his face. *She's alive and fine. Why do I keep having the nightmare?*

And why had it popped to mind when he'd been with Erica? What an arse he'd been, though not intentionally. If she'd left the lights on, maybe he'd have been looking at *her* and not gotten caught up in the memory. Bloody hell, he hoped having an orgasm wouldn't trigger the flashback. Erica was the first woman he'd been with since being infected with Darkness.

He got dressed and checked out of the motel room he'd booked just down the street from the one Erica was staying. He felt disoriented, out of sorts. Nothing new, really, since he'd been afflicted with Darkness. What *was* new was being drawn here to Strasford. Yesterday he left the house first thing in the morning for what he thought was a road trip. He followed a strong pull to this town that seemed ordinary on the surface. But something was different about this place. Not only the tremors and the foul attitude of the locals. Something pulsed here, an energy that thrummed inside him.

Today he was going out to the desert. He wanted to run, let his beast free, and find out more. The energy grew stronger on the northern edge of town. He walked into the chilly morning air to check out.

A skinny guy paced outside the office door, one hand holding a cell phone to his ear. “I’m telling you, there’s no logical reason for the tremors. I’ve studied the charts, the plates, and the seismologic data. I have a call into the NEIC. Their seismometers don’t detect anything. Not a blip. The disruption is completely localized. And I can’t find a single reason for it. I need a few more days because this is driving me crazy.”

The guy was just hanging up when Magnus emerged from the office. He paused, then decided, what the hell? “You’re a seismologist?”

“Yes.” The guy raked long, knobby fingers through his thick hair. “A frustrated one, as you can tell.”

“Let me ask you this: do you feel a dense energy in the area?” Magnus wasn’t sure how to even describe it. He flattened his hand on his chest. “Like a vibration you can feel inside?”

The guy looked up, as though to tune in. After a few seconds, he shook his head. “No, I don’t feel anything like that.”

Magnus shrugged. “Maybe it’s just me. Have a good one, mate.”

*Maybe it's just me.* It was him, he realized. Darkness. Whatever pulled him here connected to that foreign energy inside him. Drew it, and thus, him. The closer he'd gotten to Strasford, the stronger the vibration. Add the tremors, the eruptions of tempers in the last few weeks, and something was very wrong here.

Once in his car, he headed north. A glance in the rearview mirror had him thinking about Erica again. The woman in the car a few lengths back reminded him of her, though she was wearing sunglasses.

Erica had hang ups, no doubt. He'd never been with a woman who wanted sex but didn't want pleasure. He'd picked up snatches of her thoughts, first her need for the connection of sex and her attraction to him. She'd put up the boundaries: the light being off, wanting to get right down to it. But he knew she wanted more than the physical release, so he'd pushed past those boundaries by giving her the pleasure she needed on a deeper level. It had surprised her…and scared her. He felt her close up, and then he'd been hit by the flashback.

He'd sensed her relief at being able to send him away with good reason. That's what she obviously did, reached out and then pushed back. It was that need, that hint of fragility, that made him realize he just needed to go instead of try to make things right. The last thing she needed, even temporarily, was someone like him in her life.

He pulled into a small parking area for a trailhead. *WANDERING HILLS PARK*, the sign read. The trail, packed smooth dirt, did wander up into the hills covered in scrub and evergreens. He stepped out into the bright sunny morning, seeing his breath fog in the cold air. The energy thrummed even stronger here. He needed to find out what it was.

The closer he got to the source, the stronger his urge to Become. He knew when Darkness was coming but hadn't mastered control over it yet. The mountain lion was the animal he'd chosen to focus his energy into Becoming. His lion pushed against him, wanting to burst out. Jessie's dad had warned Magnus about that, but it usually happened as a result of some strong emotion. Magnus had dulled everything inside him. Or rather, the hopelessness of his situation had. Why was the drive to Become so overwhelming?

He jogged past a blond man with his backpack and walking stick.

The man waved. "Morning! Beautiful out here, isn't it?" He was way too friggin' cheery.

Magnus nodded and turned a corner, losing sight of the man. The urge to run pressed harder. He veered off the trail and into the woods. *Better duck out of sight before I Become in front of someone.*

Finding no one in sight, he let the lion loose.

Had he made her? Erica picked up her pace along the trail, hoping to spot him in the distance. She came around a bend, where the path straightened, but saw no sign of Magnus. He had to have left the trail. Which meant he was probably getting into position somewhere, waiting for the right victim. What if she walked by? Would he think it a coincidence? Would he choose her? She flexed her fingers, the scars tightening across the backs of her hands. She hoped so.

After passing a man going in the same direction, he startled her with a chipper, "Morning!"

She whirled around. "Uh, hi."

He had pale blond hair that was starting to thin, the complexion of someone with an indoor job, and the bright smile of a man who'd never been trashed by life. Or he was a good actor.

His smile faltered. "You all right?"

She forced one of her own. "Fine. I got this brilliant idea to jog down the path and remembered very quickly how out of shape I am." He couldn't see her toned body beneath her sweater and pants.

"You've got to pace yourself on these kinds of walks. Be the tortoise, not the hare. Are you searching for the mysterious black smoke, too?"

She fell into step beside him, all the while searching for Magnus. "What smoke?"

"People have been reporting a plume of smoke coming from a crack in the ground." He whipped out his compass. "Somewhere to the east. After they've seen it, they feel disoriented and fuzzy; some even reported memory loss. With all the strange behavior going on here lately, I'm going to investigate it. Maybe the tremors have opened a crack in the ground and unleashed toxic gas."

"Is that what you do, air safety?"

He chuckled. "No. I'm a preacher, actually. But I care about people. If there's a toxic leak, I want to map it so it can be investigated." He thrust out his hand. "I'm Graham."

"Erica," she said, accepting his handshake for, oh, about a second before letting go. A preacher who wanted to help mankind. Yeah, this guy could be the killer, too. "Mind if I check it out with you?"

"Not at all. I'd enjoy the company."

If this man was the real deal, what would he think if he knew she'd killed eight people? At least she killed for a reason; her quarry killed for pleasure.

Sometime later, Graham paused, consulting his map and compass. "This is where we leave the trail. The two people I spoke with have sketchy memories, but they were both certain they strayed here." He squinted as he looked into the distance. "They saw the smoke…there!"

Against the bright, clear sky, a trail of black smoke snaked up. It didn't look like ordinary smoke but was thick and almost oily.

Graham slathered on sun block, holding out the bottle when he was done.

"No, thanks." She didn't think she'd live long enough to die from something normal like that.

He stared at the trail of smoke, his jovial expression now somber. "There's something evil about it. It just feels wrong."

"I thought I was imagining it."

He touched the cross pendant at his neck. "You sure you want to go?"

"I've always been drawn to the dark side," she said, then laughed when he glanced her way. "Figuratively speaking. Let's go check it out."

She kept a comfortable distance between them as they slogged their way across the open land. An intermittent gust pelted them with sand that stung her face and hands. The wilderness spread out in all directions, making her feel isolated. Vulnerable. Yes, this was the landscape of her soul, barren and scarred and so all alone. Ever since she'd left home at sixteen.

The sun beat down on them as they closed in on the smoke, which drifted from a crack in a grouping of rocks. She detected no smell but could feel the dizzying effect Graham had described. The smoke was cooler than the air temperature and odd.

She glanced over to find him blinking. "You all right?"

"It's evil." He said the words with complete seriousness. "Like Hell's sprung a leak." He pulled out his map and made a notation, then brought out a camera and snapped some pictures.

Graham pointed to the west. "Someone's coming."

Another smoke seeker? The man stumbled into view, his clothing wrinkled, brown hair disheveled. He appeared to be in his thirties.

Graham started forward, his hand already pulling the water bottle from his hip. His hiking shoes kicked up puffs of sand. The man fell and couldn't stand after several tries. Finally he pulled himself across the sand, his breath coming in shallow gasps as he stared at the smoke. She saw no blood on him, no sign of injury. Maybe he was one of the disoriented. She remained back for a reason she couldn't quite name.

Graham dropped beside the man, tilting the bottle to his mouth and speaking words she could not hear.

It happened so fast, Erica couldn't open her mouth to warn him. The man shoved his fist toward Graham's chest. *Into* his chest. Blood sluiced out of the gaping hole. He pulled out a bloody mass and howled.

Not real. Couldn't be. The horror of it froze her even as her fingers twitched to do something. He held...held...*Graham's heart.* Her own heart stopped, the sight draining all the blood from her head and the breath from her chest. She knew the serial killer tore out hearts, but seeing it was beyond horrible.

Graham slumped back and fell to the sand.

She launched toward the carnage. Toward the man who held...God, he was holding up Graham's heart as though offering it to the sky.

His gaze snapped to her, and he smiled. "More." He shimmered, turning black. Not a mirage. He was changing form, to something that looked like a large animal.

She held her hand toward him, focusing all her fury and fear into a deadly stream of energy. Like lightning, it arced in brilliant blue, forks snaking out in all directions. Pain arced up along her arms, too, moving like fire across her existing scars. The man-thing flew back, landing several feet away. He trembled and became man again, struggling to sit up. She aimed the flow at him until his body shuddered and then stilled.

No way would her knees hold her. She crawled across the sand. *Get to Graham before it hits.* Small sounds, like grunts came from her throat. Not cries or screams, but a twisted mess of both held captive. Besides the men she'd killed, she had only witnessed death once. She would see the car hitting her childhood friend for the rest of her life, the sound of metal hitting flesh, the sight of Missy's body landing on the street. It had imprinted on her nine-year-old mind forever.

She reached Graham, feeling her stomach tumble at the sight of the gaping hole in his chest. Sand pelted her and his body as wind gusted. The bloody lump of his heart lay in the sand. No chance of helping him. She looked at the man in the near distance, also dead.

Was she having a nightmare? A psychotic break? She searched her surroundings, so normal and starkly beautiful. The shapes of the rocks and mountains in the distance didn't morph to monsters. The sand didn't writhe.

The pain hit then. She cried out, unable to still the guttural scream. Her body jerked as the Lightning rocketed through her. She called it backlash. Fire screamed up her scars again, going higher, nearly to her shoulder this time. She dug her fingers into the sand, trying to anchor her. How many times could her body withstand this? And then she couldn't think at all.

Copeland looked up as Lanna knocked on his door and then pushed it open. "What now?"

"Your brother's gone again."

"Dammit, we're too close for this crap." He checked the time. Way too close. "There's only one place he could be."

Nester had gone against the rules by tapping into the Darkness. Once they found the crack from which Darkness leaked, he couldn't resist taking more, like a drug addict, becoming mad for it. If he was found out, he'd be executed on the spot by the rest of the group. Fortunately, Copeland had earned the autonomy of being the one who monitored the effects Darkness was having on Strasford. But it was only a matter of time before Torus caught wind of the Heart Ripper and tied it to someone with Darkness. Especially after there had recently been a murder attributed to the offspring of one of the other Darkened men.

Their house sat alone at the far edge of civilization, desert and mountains stretching out beyond them. He spotted the faint plume of smoke in the distance.

"There are his tracks," Lanna said, pointing to digs in the sand.

Soon his footprints were harder to find in the wind-brushed sand, but he knew where his brother was headed.

Word had gotten out locally about the mysterious smoke, a bad thing. So far only a few had ventured out to assuage their curiosity, and the smoke hadn't always cooperated.

He wished he had teletransportation abilities. Some lucky bastards from his dimension did, but he had to slog through thirty minutes of sand and sand-spiked wind to reach his destination.

Lanna pointed at a lump on the ground. "What's that?" The wind whipped her fine blond hair across her face.

"I don't know." His chest constricted, though he couldn't say why.

As they neared, he saw another lump. Beyond them, Darkness drifted up and disappeared in the wind. He quickened his pace, his wife close behind.

They came upon the body of a man he didn't know. A human from this dimension with a hole in his chest.

"Nester." The word came out a growl. He'd attacked this man. Copeland turned to the other lump on the ground a short distance away. And obviously someone else, too.

Lanna's gasp echoed his own as they neared that body. *Nester.* Life ebbed through his being, its hum nearly nonexistent. Copeland dropped down next to his brother. "Nester!"

No response. Copeland put his hands on his chest. Was there enough life to bring him back? Something had shocked his heart. There was a scorch mark on his shirt.

"What could have done this?" Lanna checked the sky. "Lightning? But there isn't a storm cloud anywhere in sight."

"This isn't a human-inflicted wound." He surveyed the area, ready for an attack, but saw nothing. "Keep an eye out."

He used his energy to suffuse Nester's heart with healing power. Copeland could feel it quivering. Lanna knelt across from him and put her hands on Nester, too. She didn't have healing powers, but her energy would help nonetheless.

"I can feel it returning to a regular heartbeat," she said.

Their bodies weren't that different than human bodies, anatomically speaking. An unpopular theory back in their home dimension was that his species had started out as humans. For reasons unknown, a large group decided to live belowground. Being exposed to the Earth's magnetic field altered their bodies, allowing them to change form or use their energy differently than the more dense humans aboveground.

Once the humans used biological weapons to kill each other off, the Callorians, as they called themselves, had eventually returned to the surface. Their leaders decided that emotions were the downfall and convinced an entire generation to repress them. They taught their children and thus, a much simpler way of life.

When their group was dispatched to this dimension years ago, they had to generate the denser body of regular humans to blend in. They could not use their powers in public, nor were they permitted to socialize with the humans here. That was not a problem for him; he had no use for them.

Lanna watched Nester's face relax. "He'll live?" Worry creased her forehead. The more they lived in this dimension, the more emotions infected them. Lanna was beginning to want certain things from him after devouring erotic romances. Things that repulsed him.

He felt the now steady heartbeat through his fingers. "Yes. Tell me what happened here."

She stood, eyes closed and fingers flexed as she summoned the past. Her red, long nails glittered in the sunlight. She trembled as he knew images flashed through her mind. Her body tensed under the onslaught of them, her outstretched arms rigid.

"I see what looks like a bolt of lightning shoot Nester in the chest." She grimaced. "Pain, excruciating."

"It was one of our people, wasn't it? No human here has this kind of power." His brother didn't exactly endear himself to the others. Had he incited an altercation? Did anyone at the Las Vegas compound know of the leak?

"Wait. There's a woman here, too. I can feel her outrage. And her pain."

So Nester had also inflicted damage. He scanned the area for another body. "Who is she?"

"Not one of us."

A stranger. He leaned closer to her. "Did she create this injury?"

"I can't tell."

"Tell me more about her."

"She's tall, thin with shoulder-length blond hair." Lanna's face screwed up. "Wait. I sense Callorian, but I can't be sure it's her. There's such a tangle of energies. It's hard to discern. Hmm. I see another man. A big, muscular one." Her mouth tilted up a little at whatever image she was seeing.

"What about him?"

Her smile disappeared at his harsh question. "He was in the area, but I can't be sure he was here when this happened." Her eyebrows furrowed. "Hmm, that's odd."

"What? What else?"

Her eyebrows furrowed beneath her wispy bangs. "It's probably the leak interfering, but I'm picking up a lot of Callorian essence." She opened her eyes, heavy as always when she came out of the trance.

He gripped her arm. "Come, let's find them."

# CHAPTER 4

Erica slogged through the sand and searing sun. Her hands ached, her body ached, and her mind ached every time she thought about what had happened twenty minutes ago. She thought she was heading back to the trail, but she'd obviously lost her way.

The area was strewn with enormous rocks, and she walked in their shadows for relief from the sun. A sound caught her attention and shuddered through her. Any noise would set her off now, but this one sounded like a roar. Not a flesh-and-blood animal roar though. She searched the horizon. Were there more of…of whatever that man had been?

She edged closer to the rock and peered around it. In the near distance, a man raced across the top of a low, flat rock. Her heart hammered at the sight of him. Magnus. Hell, she'd forgotten all about him. He wasn't the Heart Ripper. Maybe he could help her.

Magnus reached the edge of the rock, braced his hand on it, and jumped easily to the ground several feet below. In cut-off jean shorts, sneakers, and nothing else, he ran the back of his arm across his forehead as he turned and climbed back up. Then he raced across the surface and jumped off the other end and out of sight.

He seemed to be playing. Or practicing for a race. But he radiated fierce determination by the hard set of his mouth and eyebrows. Not the charmer she'd met. His movements were jerky and sharp. *No, let's not approach the angry man tearing around the middle of nowhere.*

She walked closer to the rocks, staying in the shadows. Fear squeezed her chest at the sound of footfalls coming closer. She flexed her arms, the newly scarred skin tight and painful over her shoulders. She'd never had to use Lightning back to back. Would it work?

Would it kill her?

A black puma raced around the end of the rock and came to a stop yards from her. Not a normal cat, its body was made of churning blackness, the same as that smoke. Before she could stifle her scream, he morphed into…*Magnus*?

"Dammit," he muttered, shaking his head and making his curls bounce. "You startled me." He gave her a contrite look. "I don't suppose there's any chance you didn't see that."

She pushed out the words, "Get away from me."

He raised his hands in surrender. "I didn't think so. Look, I'm not going to hurt you."

A strangled laugh erupted from her throat. "Like your friend didn't hurt that man."

If she didn't know better, if she hadn't seen him turn from beast to man, she might believe his puzzled expression.

"I don't have any friends here." His eyebrows furrowed even more. "Someone's hurt?"

She started backing up. "Just let me leave, and I won't hurt you."

He blinked. "*You* won't hurt *me*?"

"I have a weapon. But we don't have to go there. I'll forget what I saw, and you forget about seeing me. Who'd believe me anyway?"

His gaze shifted to something behind her at the same moment her back came up against a hard body. With a yelp, she spun and stumbled away from another man. Two of them! No way could she summon strength to zap two more. Her throat closed in fear.

This man didn't look scary, with dark blond hair slicked back, even in the breeze. Still, she sensed a tightly-coiled tension in him, a fury in his gray eyes.

"Copeland! Where are—?" A woman stepped into view, paused at the sight of them, and ran over to stand next to the man. Like the Heart Ripper and the second man, she appeared to be in her early thirties, her white-blond hair ruffled from the breeze. Her sharp blue eyes scanned both her and Magnus.

"Are these the two you saw, Lanna?"

"Yes." Her gaze settled on Magnus and became almost predatory.

Copeland held out his hand toward them. "Yes, I feel what you were talking about."

Erica shrank back, not wanting him to feel anything that belonged to her. She bumped against Magnus and reflexively jerked away when he reached to steady her.

"Don't move," Copeland ordered. His gaze shifted from her to Magnus. "Which of you tried to kill my brother?" He pointed to Magnus. "You?"

"Killed? I haven't killed anyone lately."

*Lately?*

Erica turned to Magnus. What kind of game were they playing? He was obviously one of them. Admitting that she killed that awful man would be a bad thing. Wait a minute. Hadn't Copeland said 'tried to kill'? Which meant the creepy bastard wasn't dead.

She injected a confidence she didn't feel into her words. "Someone's waiting for me at my car, so I'd better go before he gets worried." She started to walk away, her breath stuck in her chest.

A hand grabbed her shoulder. "You're not going anywhere."

She jerked out of Copeland's grasp. Before she could say a word, Magnus moved closer, his face a tight mask. "Take your hands off her and let her leave. I don't know what you're into here, but I haven't hurt anyone and neither has she."

He was defending her? Or pretending to. Of course, all he'd seen of her was a woman afraid of the light so he'd think she was harmless. Needy. *Ugh.* But why pretend he wasn't with these two? If that creepy guy turned into a black beast, and so did Magnus, it had to mean they were all the same. She really had to get away from these people.

She flexed her stiff hands and nodded to Magnus. "He's right. We're not involved in whatever it is you're talking about. If I don't return within a few minutes, my friend will call the police."

"Which friend?" Copeland flicked his gaze to the man beside her. "This one? Or the one who's dead back there?"

"I don't know what you're talking about."

Copeland narrowed his eyes at her. "Oh, I think you do."

How could he possibly know that?

"You both will have to come with me. We have much to talk about. Like who you are, and how you shocked my brother's heart. Or how your friend here did it." He latched onto her arm, clenching his fingers.

Magnus muttered, "Not bloody again," and yanked the guy's hand away. "I said, let go of her and bugger off."

Copeland merely smiled. "And what will you do to stop me?"

Blackness vibrated around Magnus, and his deceptively boyish looks turned into a dark scowl. He was morphing to the puma again.

Copeland raised his hand and waved it in a circle. A fiery sensation swept through her, and all she saw was a red flash. Fire! She was surrounded by fire. Then everything went blindingly white before she lost consciousness.

# CHAPTER 5

"We'll extract the answers we need and then kill them."

Magnus stirred awake to those words. He felt completely shattered, like he'd not only been hit by a truck but then run over several times.

"What I don't understand," the man—Copeland, he suspected—continued, "is how they're Callorian."

The people from the other dimension? Well, that explained the man's ability to blast them. Pope, their Callorian ally and sort-of family, had said there were others out there.

"They're not fully Callorian," Lanna said. "But they definitely hold the essence. It baffles me, too. Maybe they'll open up to me. I'm nicer than you are."

Magnus opened his eyes and immediately found that his arms were manacled above his head. The bar stool he'd been propped up on fell as he tried to jerk away from the wall he was leaning against. He stopped it from banging on the floor with his foot, but that's when he realized his ankles were manacled too. Fear chilled him like a dunk in a barrel of ice water. He was in what looked like a small jail cell in the corner of a mostly bare basement. He saw no windows or exterior doors, only an odd steel door that was rounded at the top. In the corner, a set of concrete stairs went up. What he didn't see were Copeland and Lanna. Hadn't he just heard them or was it a dream?

Copeland's voice echoed from a vent in the ceiling. "See what you can find out. I'm leaving in thirty minutes."

"You mean *we're* leaving."

"You have to stay here with Nester. And to keep an eye on our prisoners."

"You're leaving me out of the robbery? That's not fair." Lanna's petulance was clear. "We've been planning this for weeks. Can't we do it tomorrow?"

"We don't have time to wait. You know that. We need to grab as much cash as we can if we're going to set up new lives here."

Magnus's restraints were attached to the stone wall, and no amount of pulling even budged them. He summoned Darkness, knowing his lion would have a lot more strength. Except…he couldn't Become.

Copeland's first words echoed in Magnus's mind: Extract answers and kill them.

*Them.*

Magnus found Erica lying on the concrete floor a few feet away. Stilling the panic that she was dead, he watched for the gentle rise and fall of her chest. Yes, alive. Since the cell was only set up for one prisoner, they'd used a standard handcuff to secure her to one of the bars. She was coming awake, too, going through the same process of realization that he'd just done.

Panic suffused her expression as she jerked fully awake, more so when she realized she was cuffed. She stood, her legs shaky, sliding the cuff along the bar as high as it would go. Her gaze flew to him. “Why are *you* restrained, too?” She was obviously confused to see him in the same position as herself. “Did they turn on you?”

A door opened at the top of the steps, and Copeland came down, Lanna following. She looked unhappy. Magnus tried to sort through what he’d overheard. They were planning a robbery. And she’d said they were Callorian. He *and* Erica. What the hell?

Copeland assessed the two of them, his gaze stopping on Magnus. “One of you tried to kill my brother, and I want to know who and how. You both have something in you that interests me greatly.”

Magnus wasn’t feeling particularly cooperative. “I don’t know what you’re talking about.”

“I think you do.” Copeland unlocked the cell door and stepped inside, Lanna right behind him. “There’s something different about you. I’m sure you’ve realized it by now. You have a special ability. Yet you are mostly human from this dimension. Magnus McLeod, you will tell me how you came to have this. And how you came to Hold Darkness.”

They knew his name. Of course, after he’d zapped him, they’d searched his pockets and found his wallet. He didn’t let on that hearing his name had any effect, but it bugged the hell out of him. He focused on the fact that they knew what Darkness was.

“Special ability? Well, I’m especially good with the ladies. I can keep a hard-on for hours. Is that what you mean?”

Copeland flicked a glance to the manacles. “You’re in no position to be coy.”

"Coy, hell, I'm answering your question. What do you mean by Darkness?"

"You don't ask the questions." Copeland punched him in the stomach. Magnus didn't have time to tighten his muscles and took it deep. "Care to share now?"

Yeah, right after he upchucked all over the guy's black leather shoes. Pain radiated through his stomach, doubling him over.

Copeland seemed pleased with his big show of strength. "I suppose you don't know what it's called."

"Is that supposed to be an apology?"

"Hardly. You can summon a dark energy we call Darkness to change your form. Don't deny it. I saw you try earlier. You cannot do it now, however, as the metal of your cuffs won't allow it. This is a detainment system for my brother when he goes mad. The metal curtails your ability, one you will now share with me."

Magnus studied the metal, seeing that it had a sheen to it he'd never seen before. And he realized he'd not picked up anyone's thoughts either. All right, he'd give the son of a bitch an ability. "I can astral project, send my soul to another location." It wasn't something he used often.

"And what about Darkness?"

He would never give away Jessie's existence. "I walked in on a fight between two men a couple of weeks ago. I tried to intervene, and one turned into a black beast and tore my throat. When I came to, I was whole, only my dried blood to prove that it hadn't been some horrible dream. But I felt different after that. If something riles me, my body starts to turn into something else. I don't know what it's called or what it even is. I thought it was something like werewolves, where I've been infected. What is it?"

Erica was listening intently to every word he said, the horror of it clear on her expression.

Lanna started to answer, but Copeland cut her off. "It's a dark energy, as I said. There are some who have tapped into it. Apparently one healed you. Where did this occur?"

"Minnesota, on a camping trip." He wanted them nowhere near Annapolis. Near his brother, Jessie, or their friends.

Copeland turned his attention to Erica. "And what about your girlfriend here?"

"She's not my girlfriend. We don't even know each other." He wanted to make that clear so the asshole wouldn't use her to torment answers out of him. He would not give away that they'd had whatever it was they'd had.

"I don't become a dark beast," Erica said.

"No, but you have a special ability, don't you?"

"Yeah, I write fiction. I create terrible people who murder for fun and then I kill them off."

Lanna stepped up beside Copeland, slipping her arm around his. "You both have the Callorian essence. How can it be that you don't know each other?"

Copeland slid out of her grasp, a subtle rebuff. "Too much of a coincidence to believe. Especially as we caught you together."

Magnus looked at Erica again, her messy blond hair, lean face, and haunted blue eyes. She was keeping her cool, he'd give her that. But she clearly had no idea what they were talking about.

Lanna studied them. “I don’t sense any attachment between them.”

“You’re gullible,” Copeland bit out. “You saw the way he stepped in to protect her.”

Lanna walked up to Magnus, giving him a sweeping once-over. “I think he’s just that kind of human. Something we don’t see a lot of.” She drew her finger from his collarbone down the center of his bare chest. “I want to keep him.”

“Lanna,” Copeland growled. “Take your hands off him. He’s not a *pet*.”

She stepped away but kept that heated gaze on him. “It’s only for a couple of days, until…” She gave Copeland a knowing look.

The idea of being her pet held appeal only because it would give him a chance to escape. He was more concerned about what she hadn’t said.

Copeland grabbed Erica’s hand, pushing her sleeve back to expose a forearm covered in fine scars. “Interesting scars, Erica.” She tried to pull away but he held her firmly as he turned her palm upward to reveal a red mark right in the center. “There are people, our people, who can wield a power called the Flare. It’s a shot of high voltage electricity that comes from the palm.” He rubbed his thumb over the red mark. “If you were wholly Callorian, your body would tolerate that kind of energy. Your feeble human body cannot. It’s very painful when you use it, isn’t it? It was painful when you used it on my brother.”

Her mouth tightened. She wanted to say something, but not the answer he was seeking. Interesting. Did she try to kill the bastard’s brother? Could she be deadly? When she’d seen him turn from Darkness to human, she'd said, *Just leave me alone and I won't hurt you.* Which had seemed a humorous threat at the time. Magnus had pegged her as lonely and insecure, but there was a lot more to her than that. He hadn't noticed the scars, but then again, they'd been naked in the dark. Pope had an ability like that, before he'd been psychically handcuffed.

Copeland released her at last. "The man we found dead wasn't Callorian. I'll wager you were with him when my brother attacked. He has a nasty habit of pulling out people's organs." He made mock *tsking* sounds. "It's an annoying predilection to say the least. It must have been quite disconcerting to see your friend, perhaps boyfriend, having his heart wrested from his chest. Was it still beating while Nester held it?"

Her reaction gave away her knowledge of the macabre event Copeland described. Admirably, she held onto the control he was trying to crack.

"That's what I thought." He grabbed her chin so hard, his fingers dug into her skin. "So you electrocuted him, didn't you?"

Magnus pulled against his manacles. "Let her go!" Darkness pulled and twisted inside him, but the cold metal remained tight against his wrists—his very human wrists. He saw the remnants of horror on Erica's face at watching his efforts to transform.

*Beast*. He didn't have to hear her thoughts to know that's what she was thinking when she looked at him.

Copeland released her, but his gaze was on Magnus. "I know why *you're* here. The Darkness pulled you, called to you. That's what happened to my brother. He found where Darkness is seeping out of the earth and started taking it in like a drug. It's making him quite crazy."

Something *had* called to Magnus. But the Darkness wasn't here; it was in the other dimension, according to Jessie's dad, who had tapped into it years earlier. Then he had come here through a portal.

"It did pull me here." Magnus had to word what he said about Darkness carefully, since he was playing dumb.

"And it turns you into *monsters*." Erica was looking at Magnus on that last word.

The alarm on Copeland's watch beeped. "I have to go."

Lanna's face hardened, but she held in whatever it was that she wanted to say. Her job was to get more answers out of them. She followed Copeland up the stairs, arms crossed over her chest.

As soon as the door closed, Erica asked, "Who are you? *What* are you?"

"You got us into this mess, and you're hammering *me* with questions? You've got to be kidding me."

"What do you mean, *I* got us into this?"

Magnus nodded toward the vent and leaned as close as he could. "Lower your voice. They can hear us through that vent. Or at least I could hear them, so I figure it works both ways. Come closer so we can talk."

She actually reared back, her eyes narrowing in suspicion.

"Do you want answers or not?"

She did, enough to relent and lean toward him.

"You tried to kill that bloke's brother with the Flare he was talking about. Some kind of power you've had since you were, say, a teenager, I bet. When I came up on you, you held out your hand like you were going to zap me into tomorrow." He looked at the crisscross scarring across the back of the hand he could see.

She shifted so her body blocked her hand, but her eyes had widened at his words. This lass could kill. It raised some questions of his own. But first he had to gain her trust, because she wasn't going to tell him a thing before that.

He went on. "Let me guess. Your mother or father died while working for the government in a covert program."

She maintained a guarded expression but gave him a subtle nod.

"Aye, it's all beginning to make sense now."

"What is?"

"Why I was drawn to you at the bar." The same way he'd been drawn to Jessie. He thought it was his imagination. "When I walked past you, didn't I feel different from all those other men you pick up?"

She winced.

"Sorry, that didn't come out the way I'd intended. But let's be honest; neither one of us is unused to the idea of sleeping with a stranger, eh? We both needed something the other could provide. Hell, I don't even know your last name. Which is?"

"None of your damned business."

She had a tough shell, but something in her blue eyes said there was a good reason why. It was the same pain he'd seen after their disastrous encounter. She wasn't after a tumble in the sack for fun. He still felt bad for spoiling it.

"Look, Erica, we're on the same side. We—"

"We are not on the same side. You're some kind of beast that can rip out a person's heart while it's still beating!" Her voice cracked, broke, and her body trembled.

"So you admit to at least seeing the guy. Copeland's brother killed your boyfriend, and you zapped him."

"He wasn't my boyfriend; he was a preacher out to find the mysterious smoke. I tagged along. You can't imagine what it was like, seeing his heart in that man's hands. The blood. The gloating look on his face. Then he saw me." Terror painted her expression. "And he said, 'More.'"

How the hell did he keep getting tangled up with women who were in trouble? First Jessie, who'd nearly gotten him killed, and now this lass, who'd inadvertently gotten him imprisoned. Still, the need to protect her pulsed through him at the thought of her facing a monster like that.

*She thinks you're a monster, too.*

He said, "I don't blame you for zapping him. It saved your life."

She hung her head low. "I should have done it faster to save Graham."

He gripped the chain that held the cuffs to the wall and pulled it from every angle. No give. "I saw my mother get killed, and I thought the same thing for a long time. *If.* If I'd moved faster, done something, maybe I could have saved her."

She looked up at that, shock on her face. "Your mother died in front of you?"

He nodded. No need to say that it was his own brother who had pushed a sword into her stomach, locked in a mental time warp and fighting British soldiers. His addiction to astral projection made him temporarily crazy. "You can't change the past, no matter how many times you relive it. No way could you have seen that coming. Then I probably scared the hell out of you again."

"I assumed you were one of them. Not a stretch, considering."

"I suppose not. But the truth is we have more in common than you want to admit. We have special abilities because of that program I mentioned." He studied the chain, searching for any weakness in the links. "If I knew your last name, I could tell you for sure."

After a few moments, she said, "Evrard."

He knew it, and a few seconds later it came to him. "You're Jerryl's sister?"

Something frosty flowed through her eyes, even as she looked surprised. "You know my brother?"

"Of him. He worked for Darkwell, the man responsible for the deaths of almost everyone in that program. Of course, Jerryl didn't know that," he added at the shock on her face. "I'm sure he thought he was on the right side." Magnus worked on the bolt that held his cuffs to the wall while he talked. "It was the government, after all. But Darkwell was corrupt."

"When my father called to tell me he was dead, he went on about some secret project Jerryl was involved in. He missed the irony that our mother died doing the same kind of thing, leaving behind a whole lot of questions." Her expression opened just a little. "You know about the program?"

"Aye. My father was in it, too. Darkwell recruited people with psychic gifts to spy on our enemies. Dad studied slime molds and was especially fascinated with *pwdre ser,* the slime that meteorites leave behind. One day what he collected was actually the remains of someone from the other dimension."

"Dimension?" she asked. "Like a parallel dimension?"

"Exactly. It's called Surfacia. This bloke accidentally flew his aircraft through one of the portals between dimensions and crashed. His brother cleaned up the site, but apparently he missed some. My intrepid father found it and ended up ingesting his Essence. He discovered it enhanced the psychic abilities he already had. Darkwell then gave it to the program's subjects, who eventually went crazy and had to be terminated before the public found out. You inherited that Essence—and, I suspect, the bloke's ability. Recently, Darkwell started recruiting the subjects' offspring to resurrect the program. I'm sorry to say your brother was killed because he worked for the man behind that program."

"I hope he burns in hell."

"No doubt Darkwell will for everything he's done."

"I mean my brother." She turned away, which was good because Magnus couldn't have been more shocked by her response.

He wanted to know why someone would hate their sibling that much, but he didn't have time to delve into her troubled psyche. "Do you remember anything when they brought us here?"

“No.” She followed his gaze as he scoured the cell they were in. “A blinding flash went through me as hot as fire and then nothing until I woke here. You?”

“The same.” His gaze lighted on the toilet and sink in the far corner. How they were supposed to use them while manacled, he didn’t know. He had good aim, but really. “We’re in a basement, I think.”

“Why would they have a jail cell in their basement?” The implications of that shadowed her eyes. “Only people who regularly kidnap and torture others would have something like this.”

“I can’t think it has anything to do with the robbery they’re planning.”

“Robbery?”

“I overheard them talking about it as I came to.”

“Oh, great, so they’re not only aliens from another dimension but common criminals.” She shook her head. “We are so screwed.”

“Well, no need to give up just yet.”

She shook her manacled hand. “Oh, don’t worry, I have loads of hope.”

Her hopelessness and fear tugged at him. No matter how hardened she was, he’d seen her vulnerable side, the pain in her eyes when she’d asked him to leave her motel room. He’d been inside her in the most intimate way and yet hadn’t connected with her. That bothered him.

There were a lot of things about her that bothered him. One, however, surged above the rest.

“You being out there in the same area I was, at the same time…that *is* a coincidence that’s hard to believe. What were you doing out there?” He studied her carefully masked face. “You were following me. Why?”

She clamped her mouth shut, avoiding his gaze.

“Were you going to punish me for calling out another lass’s name, zap me with your Flare? Are you some kind of psycho revenge bitch?”

“No.” She shook her head. “I was madder at myself than you, in any case.”

“Why?”

“It’s not important. None of it is now that we’re going to die.”

“You were stalking me then? You became obsessed, couldn’t get me out of your mind.”

She laughed though there was no humor in it. “Hardly. And I don’t call it my ‘Flare.’ I call it Lightning.”

Now he was sure she’d been following him, but he was also sure she wasn’t about to tell him why. Though it bugged him like a chigger itch, he focused on questions she was more likely to answer. “Why didn’t you use it on Copeland?”

She flexed her hand, staring at her palm. “I can’t use it twice in a row, apparently. And it’s painful. But this cuff is made of the same metal yours is.”

“How well do you know how to use your power?”

Something fierce lit her eyes. “Very well.”

He had no idea what he was getting into with her. But he wasn’t going to let her give up hope.

# CHAPTER 6

Erica was in the grip of a drug-induced nightmare. There was no other explanation. She'd had sex with a hunky stranger who laced her drink with LSD, and she was now lying inert on her bed while he did God-knew-what to her body. And that was far better than this version of reality.

She could believe that if she couldn't feel the bite of the cuff around her wrist, the scrape of the stone wall at her back. If this didn't feel so dreadfully real.

A lone set of footsteps sounded down the stairs, and her whole being tightened. Lanna came into view with a bright, anticipatory expression and stepped up to the bars. Erica wondered if the woman always had that carnal light in her eyes. At least she seemed to when she looked at Magnus. Lanna unlocked the door, stepped inside, and locked it again.

"I'm sorry that my husband hit you the way he did," she said, walking close to Magnus. He said nothing, regarding her warily.

She pulled a tube from her pocket, her gaze on the ripped muscles of his stomach. "Black Lavender, from my dimension. It's amazing for healing pain. You've got a bruise," she said, pouting. "He's a mean man. So

Callorian. But you, you're much more *human.*" She feathered her fingers across his abs. "You've got *heat.*"

Heat. The way she said the word *sounded* hot. Sensual. Erica took in the expanse of his stomach, too, the emerging bruise, his ribs, wide and deep, and the way his waist tapered to slim hips. She hadn't let herself touch him beyond the necessary contact. But she'd wanted to.

Lanna squeezed out some dark purple gel from the tube and rubbed it across his skin. She was mesmerized by him, moving her hand in slow circles, as though she'd never touched a man before. She probably hadn't touched a purely human male, and Magnus was a beautiful specimen, after all.

"Just like in the books I read. Strong, sexy, and you smell so good." Lanna breathed him in, her eyes closed. "We don't sweat like you do. It's a provocative scent."

The violation shuddered through Erica. But something sensual stirred beneath that, and she was disgusted by it.

"What kind of books do you read, Lanna?" he asked, his voice level and normal, as though one participant of the conversation wasn't shackled to a wall.

"Erotic ones. *Fifty Shades*. BDSM. Spanking. And lots of sex. Whenever we go into town, I visit the romance section of the bookstore. Humans like having sex. They like touching, breathing in, tasting."

Not all humans, Erica thought.

Lanna perched on her tiptoes and ran her tongue down his neck.

His body tensed. "I don't think your husband would be very pleased to find you like this."

"No, he wouldn't." The thought of that obviously doused her heat for a moment. "Callorians don't have sex for fun. We procreate, we release, but we don't play."

Oh, God, Erica *was* part…whatever the hell they were. Sex for release, nothing more. *No, you've just been damaged.*

Lanna pressed her body against his and nuzzled his neck. "I want to play. With you."

Magnus's gaze found Erica, sending a flush over her cheeks. "It's not right, Lanna. Your husband nearby, Erica right here, having to watch."

Lanna flicked her a provocative look. "Maybe she likes to watch."

Erica's cheeks flamed hotter. "It's disgusting and wrong to force yourself on someone else."

Magnus met her gaze on her vehement words.

Lanna laughed, deep and hearty, and gracefully waved her hand Vanna White style toward the ridge in Magnus's shorts. "It's not forcing when he likes it." She turned back to Magnus, a smile on her face. "You do like it, don't you?"

He shrugged. "A man's body reacts."

Lanna obviously didn't take it as the noncommittal answer that it was. She ran her mouth down the center of his chest, kissing across his stomach. One of her hands snaked behind him and squeezed his ass. "You taste like fresh air and desert. And *man*."

Erica squeezed her eyes closed, wanting to shut it out. The smacking of moist lips against skin lured them open again. Magnus's jean shorts were loose enough to gap at the waistband but tight over his hips and derriere.

A tendril of desire spiraled through her, even though the hands sliding over the denim weren't hers.

What the hell was wrong with her? *She* didn't read bondage stories.

"See, she likes watching," Lanna said, flicking a glance at Erica again. "I can feel her excitement, among other things. Some people get turned on by watching another couple have sex." She pushed to her full height and up on her tiptoes, even with Magnus's face again. "Let's turn her on."

Magnus's eyes met hers, and Erica realized he'd been looking at her a lot more than he'd looked at the woman who was actually touching him.

"I don't like an audience when I'm making love to a woman," he said. "And while bondage, in theory, sounds like a great idea, having no feeling in your hands is a bit of a turn off. Half the fun of sex is feeling someone touching you; the other half is doing the touching. So you see, Lanna, we would both be cheated."

Ah, he was trying to lure her into releasing his arms.

Lanna stepped back. "As intriguing and delicious as you look there, you're right. And I do want to feel your hands on me. I've never been touched like the men in those stories touch the women." She pinned Erica with her frosty eyes. "Is that how men touch women here?"

Erica couldn't help the widening of her eyes as Lanna approached to her. "I wouldn't know; I don't read those books."

"But you've been with a man, haven't you?" Lanna was standing too close. "You've had a man touch your breasts, slide his hands all over your body, plunge his finger inside your vagina and move it just so, grinding his thumb into your clit until your whole body shudders in complete ecstasy. Had a man need you so badly that he pushes you against the wall and thrusts his pulsing rod of manhood into you right then and there?"

Erica shook her head. "Those are fantasies. Want to know what's real? Most men only care about getting off. They might squeeze your breasts and tell you how beautiful you are. The next thing you know, they're knocking on your door. In and out, and it's all over. He rolls over and turns on the television. Or makes an excuse and leaves."

Magnus's eyebrow lifted at that. Yeah, she knew he'd tried to pleasure her. She'd been the one to ask him to leave. *I'm not talking about my sex life. If that's what you want to call it.* She was relaying what she'd heard women talking about over their lattes or glasses of wine. The guy in the easy chair with the beer belly, Bud in one hand, remote in the other.

Lanna crossed her arms in front of her chest. "That's how the men in my dimension are. *Utilitarian.* But there must be men like those in the books." She shifted her attention back to Magnus. "You're not like that, like how she described, are you?"

Again, Magnus was looking at Erica. "When a woman leaves my bed, she has been thoroughly loved up one side of her body and down the other."

Erica shivered and turned away. He would have done that to her. If she'd let him. But what he'd done…oh, yeah, he wasn't lying.

Lanna's voice dropped lower. "Will you spank me? I like how a man throws a woman over his knees and spanks her bare ass. Then you can—"

"Lanna." She whirled around to find Copeland coming into view.

He had come down very quietly. "Just as I suspected. What did I tell you about cozying up to him?"

She quickly exited the cell and locked it behind her, a woman cowed. But her lascivious spirit wasn't. "He's a living, breathing manifestation of the men in those books. I can't resist." She slid the tube of gel into her pocket. "I think it's cruel to leave his hands above his head where the blood drains away."

"Why make them comfortable? I'd like to find out more about how they came to have our Essence, but only for my own curiosity. As soon as Nester comes around, he's going to want revenge on the person who zapped him." Copeland's hard gaze slid to Erica. "For once I won't mind him digging into their chests, since it won't be splashed all over the paper." He shook his head, a sneer twisting his mouth. "The Heart Ripper."

Erica could already feel a hole in her chest at the words and memory of what he'd done to Graham.

Lanna walked up to Copeland and put her hands on his shoulders. "Darling, I have a better idea for them. Well, for him, anyway."

"You can't have him for your love slave." He picked her hands from his shoulders but gripped them hard. His eyes blinked several times. "You've been touching him." Not a question.

"I put some gel on the bruise you left."

"You did more than that, you wanton bitch." He slapped her so hard she stumbled as she cupped her cheek.

Erica saw Magnus wince and tense. Was he reacting on some ingrained instinct to protect a woman, any woman? He'd tried to protect her, too.

"Lanna, you know how much is at stake here," Copeland hissed. "Our plan isn't going to work if I can't depend on the two people at my side. I wasn't gone for three minutes, and you're down here acting out your filthy books. When everything happens, you will leave them here in the house to be destroyed. They're corrupting you."

That thought sent a ripple of fear over Lanna's expression, but she wiped it away and replaced it with a contrite one. "I'm sorry."

"Yes, you are. Go up and tend to Nester. You know how he can be after he's had a hit of Darkness." Copeland gestured for her to precede him up the stairs. He closed the door with a hard clang.

Magnus banged his head back against the wall. "They're bloody mad. We have to get out of here."

She laughed softly, shaking her head. "You're good. I'll give you that. I was too easy."

"Aye, you were. You should have made me work for it. Why didn't you?"

"Maybe I was just horny. Like her." She nodded toward the door.

He regarded her in a way that made her uncomfortable. "If that's all it was, you would have let me make you come twenty ways from Sunday instead of insisting on getting right to the act. You needed something, but it wasn't just sex."

"Stop analyzing me. What are you, a drummer psychologist? Or is it that you're a sex fiend who even sinks so low he'll seduce one of our captors."

Instead of reacting, he laughed. "You're just mad because, for some reason, watching her grope me was a turn on."

"It was not! It was disturbing on so many levels."

"You were disturbed, aye, but you were more than that. It got you hot and bothered, and that's what you found most disturbing."

"Which makes me wonder, why were you looking at me the whole time? Your body was reacting, so it obviously liked what she was doing."

God, she sounded like a jealous shrew.

"Because I was imagining it was your hands on me."

Those words slammed her right in the chest. Was he kidding? Poking fun at her? "That's even more disturbing. Why weren't you imagining this Jessie you're obviously hung up on?"

He merely grunted, pulling again at the chains. "What I can't figure out is why watching another woman touch me was a turn on when you couldn't bring yourself to touch me *while we were having sex*. But you wanted to touch me." He twisted to face the wall and climbed up a couple of steps. Bracing against the wall, he pushed away. "You're a bloody enigma," he ground out.

He'd driven right through her armor down to her bone. She remembered him saying how it was better if she despised him because there was something wrong with him. Now she knew what that was. "No, Magnus, I'm just messed up. But it sounds like I won't be having that problem for much longer. You, however, have a chance."

He looked over at the sharpness in her voice, something she hadn't intended. "If that's what it takes. Wouldn't you, to survive?"

"I don't have any options."

"You make it sound like you think I'd leave you behind."

"Of course you would. Why would you risk taking the extra time to rescue me? People don't work that way."

"You don't know me very well. I wouldn't leave you."

She leaned against the wall, tilting her head up. He might feel all noble now, but the moment he was free, he would bolt. And she would be here to face their wrath alone.

# CHAPTER 7

Suza Morgan pulled into Strasford's downtown section without a moment to spare. Actually, she was one minute late, but her best friend from childhood knew she tended to run behind. Carlene had sounded odd on the phone the last two times they'd talked. Her usually bubbly friend said she felt "off" and depressed and didn't know why.

Suza decided it was time to take a road trip out to see her. She didn't have many close friends, so those she did were important to her. After spotting The Purple Fox, the health bistro Carlene raved about, Suza lucked into a parking spot near the entrance. The sign sported a purple fox holding a tomato.

"Please let this place offer something besides black bean burgers and sprouts. I really hate sprouts."

She checked herself in the rearview mirror, fluffing her straight, dark bangs and finger-combing her long hair. A tall man, his shaved head reflecting the sunlight, snagged her attention. Her heart did a silly *pitter-patter* even as she saw that it wasn't Pope. Not tall enough, broad-shouldered enough, handsome or unusual enough.

"Enough! You have to stop thinking about that man. You met him in September, and he hasn't been out to visit in the six months since. Get the hint, girl."

She didn't take it personally. He had some kind of dangerous job that kept him busy. They'd met briefly—and embarrassingly—when she'd heard her sexy client, Cheveyo, returning home while she was cleaning his house. In her impulsive, half-assed thinking, she'd posed on the back of his couch in her leopard bra and panties, planning to seduce the guy with the good heart. Then he'd walked in with his girlfriend and another man. Pope.

After she'd hastily gotten dressed, she'd been introduced to the woman who clearly had a psychic connection to Cheveyo and the tall, handsome man with the shaved head. She sensed a good heart in Pope, too, and something indefinable and different that sucked her in right along with his freaky light-violet eyes.

They'd talked on the phone several times since he'd left Arizona. Well, she talked, and he listened. Really listened, as no other man ever had. He cheered in his understated way when she told him she was able to let most of her cleaning clients go to focus on her flourishing boutique. He seemed to enjoy her stories about her quirky customers, her life, and even the wreck of her past romances.

She sighed and pushed open her door. "You've really got to stop thinking about him."

As she stepped up on the curb, a man bumped into her and then glared at *her*! "Excuse you," she said and continued on.

"What's that supposed to mean, bitch?"

The poison in his words had her spinning around. He looked nice and normal, but he felt wrong. Of course, he was snarling at her but it went way beyond that. He carried a dark, heavy energy that shot the hairs on her arms straight up.

*Not the time to be sassy.* "I said, 'Excuse me.'"

She turned back to the bistro, using the glass's reflection to keep an eye on the man. If he made a move, she was ready to use the point of her turquoise boot to introduce his balls to his kidneys. At five-foot-ten, she could kick ass if she needed to. He stared at her as though he were considering going after her. Over nothing! She lunged for the handle and stepped inside, facing him from inside. He stalked away, his body tense and rigid.

She'd sensed that dark energy just last week in a man who was staying at Cheveyo's house. Magnus had been gorgeous, polite, staying out of her way while she cleaned, but that eerie energy had wigged her out.

This was where it paid off to sense people's energy and moods. Most of the time, it was a pain in the ass.

"Table for one?" a woman asked from behind her.

Suza spun around and nearly choked at sensing the same energy in the petite hostess. Except she was smiling, though the smile didn't reach her eyes.

"I'm meeting someone." Suza searched the room full of tables. "There she is. Thanks."

Carlene stood and waved, wearing one of her kitschy cat sweaters. Her blond hair was frazzled, and she wore no makeup. Suza held out her arms to embrace her but paused. Oh, no, she had the energy, too.

"What's the matter?" Carlene asked. "You look like you saw a monster." Then she laughed. "Oh, it's me, isn't it?"

Suza blinked, speechless at the admission.

"I just didn't feel like putting on makeup or doing anything with myself. But look at you, that peaches-and-cream complexion I'd kill for, as beautiful as ever."

Suza completed their hug, holding her close for a moment. "Something strange is going on in this town."

Carlene stepped back. "You feel it? Well, of course you would." She gestured for Suza to sit and took her own seat.

"What's going on around here?"

"Tremors. Earthquake tremors. We've been experiencing them for the last month, and they're getting worse. Everyone's on edge. We've had fights, road rage, domestic violence. Even a serial killer. It's like Strasford has reverted to the Wild West days."

"Yeah, some guy was about to tear my throat out, and *he* bumped into *me*." But this wasn't just tension. She stared into her friend's eyes. "How are you feeling?"

"Tired. No, more like run down. I feel hopeless and I don't know why. My job's going good, even if my boss has been a butthead lately."

"You haven't been angry? Had any violent outbursts?" A little worrisome considering Carlene's comment about killing her over her complexion.

Carlene laughed and picked up her menu. "Of course not. You know me, still a…what was it you used to call me when you were trying to rile me up? A dishrag?"

"Only trying to urge you to stand up for yourself." Suza had no appetite, but she perused the menu. Or pretended to. Instead she checked out the bistro's patrons. Holy hell. Most had the same dark energy.

The waitress's arrival jarred her out of her freaked-out thoughts. Suza ordered the first thing her eyes found, stir-fried tofu nuggets, and focused on her friend again. Except Carlene was looking beyond her to the entrance with a blank expression and pushing to her feet. "Excuse me."

A man stepped outside, holding the door for Carlene. He appeared to be in his thirties with pale skin and blond hair combed straight back. He spoke to her for a minute, handed her a tote bag, and then she simply headed down the sidewalk beside him. No wave to Suza, no *I'll be right back.* Suza launched to her feet and made it out the door in time to see Carlene walk into the Strasford Bank right behind the man.

Suza followed in Carlene's footsteps, spotting the man exiting the bank a moment later and crossing the street. Angry shouts drew Suza closer, where several people were fighting in the bank's lobby. The security guard stood near the door like a statue, completely ignoring the scene. Two women were bickering over deposit slips at the island counter. Suza spotted her friend—holding a gun to the teller! A squeak came out of her mouth. Now the security guard took action—to keep Suza from entering the bank.

"You cannot enter here." He had that same blank look Suza had seen in the others, and they all had the dark, evil energy.

"Carlene!" she shouted, trying to maneuver around the guard.

Carlene turned, but not in response to Suza's shout. She was a zombie, clutching the tote Suza suspected contained cash and heading toward the door. In her other hand she held the gun.

The guard opened the friggin' door for her!

The alarm pealed as Carlene bumped past Suza and headed across the street. Suza grabbed her sleeve, and Carlene pointed the gun at her. "Leave me alone," she intoned like a robot. Then she turned and continued on, where she approached the man she'd spoken with earlier. She handed him the bag and walked away.

Down the road, another alarm pealed. Another zombie'd person, a young man this time, came down the sidewalk and handed the man his satchel. Then another woman came out of a jewelry store and handed the man a box. He said not one word as he took each parcel and then disappeared around the corner.

A moment later, two police cars came screaming down the road, splitting off in two directions: to each of the banks. The teller who'd handed Carlene the satchel stood by the door, one of the few people who weren't in a fugue state.

She pointed to Carlene. "That's her!"

Suza was only a few feet behind them as they approached Carlene, guns out.

"Drop the weapon!" they both shouted.

Carlene blinked, looking as though she'd just woken up. She stared at the gun, then the cops, and dropped it. They rushed in, shoving her to the ground and cuffing her.

"Wait!" Suza ran up to them, but the younger cop held out his weapon toward her.

"Back up, ma'am."

"That's my friend. She's not a bank robber." The mere notion made a hysterical giggle erupt. But she had seen it. She also saw that both cops harbored the same dark energy. Hell. Literally, like hell had crept into this lovely town.

"She's been identified as one. The only thing you can do for her is call a lawyer." He hauled her to her feet and pushed her toward the patrol car. The other cop entered the bank, which was still in a state of chaos. People inside pushed and shouted at each other as though they were oblivious to what had just happened.

Because they were.

Three more police cars joined the scene, one breaking off toward the other bank. Then the jewelry store's alarm added to the cacophony.

Suza approached the car in which Carline sat, looking shell-shocked. Her eyes met Suza's, her voice muffled by the glass of the closed window. "What happened? Why was I holding a gun?"

"You just robbed a bank."

Suza saw the shock on her friend's face.

"Move away from the car, ma'am," one of the officers shouted from the bank's entrance.

"She was in a trance," Suza said, approaching him. "Like she'd been hypnotized. She handed the money to a man."

"You're saying that your friend robbed a bank and just handed off the money? Then stood there while we arrived on the scene?"

"Yes, that's exactly what happened. Look around. These people are all in some kind of trance."

He glanced around, but Suza could see that deadened look in his eyes, too. The same way Carlene's eyes had appeared before she'd gone off with that man. "Everyone looks fine to me. Please remain nearby so we can take your statement."

Suza took a step back. "Sure. I'll do that."

What was that movie where the aliens took over people's bodies and then hunted down everyone who hadn't been infected? *Body Snatchers?*

She hated to leave her friend, but she needed to find help. Who could she call?

Why Pope's name popped into her head, she didn't know. Well, maybe because she'd been thinking about him. Because if he had a dangerous job, that meant he was used to dealing with dangerous people.

She got into her car and maneuvered out of the snarl of cars and people now crowding into the downtown area. More than half of the people had that same dull look and dark energy.

Alien invasion? Demon possession? It was going to sound crazy to Pope, but if she could get him out here, he'd see for himself.

She pulled off the road once she cleared the area and called him. "Pope, it's Suza."

"Is everything all right? You feel—er, sound, upset."

Her voice trembled with every word. "More like freaked out." She gave him a rundown of what had happened. "And the strangest part is Cheveyo's friend had a similar feel about him. Not tranced out, but dark."

"Magnus," he confirmed, oddly not reacting to her assertion. "Where is this town?"

"You don't think I'm nuts?" Relief suffused her. She thought she'd have to wheedle and convince him.

"I have quite the open mind about things of a bizarre nature."

"I'm in Strasford, in the northwest corner of Arizona. Not far from where we met in Flag."

She heard noise, and then what sounded like the crinkling of a map. "Ah."

"Ah, what?"

Silence for a moment. "You must be aware of the places of strange energy out there. Sedona has the Bell Tower, for instance. The people I work for have been investigating those areas for some time. Strasford isn't far from one of them."

Who did he work for? Questions crowded into her mind about the mysterious Pope, but the biggest one she spoke aloud: "Does this mean you're coming out?" More than relief bombarded her at the thought of seeing him again, of having him help her figure this out.

"I, uh, no, I'm afraid I can't leave my current location in Maryland. My brother, however, is very close to you. I'll ring up Cassius and send him your way. You'll be hearing from him soon."

"Will you come out at all?"

"I'm sorry, Suza. I cannot."

She released a breath. "All right, thanks for sending Cassius out." What kind of name was that? "I'll be waiting for his call."

"Go somewhere safe. Talk to no one, not even the police."

She smiled. He cared about her, dammit. That's what frustrated her the most. "I will. And won't." She remained in her car, twisting her silver rings on her trembling fingers and waiting for the phone to ring.

# CHAPTER 8

Pope studied the map for another minute. Strasford was situated between two finestras, portals to the dimension he used to call home before he became an outlaw. That couldn't be a coincidence.

He called Magnus's cell phone to see if he'd sensed anything, especially considering what Suza had said about the energy being similar to his. No answer. Then he called Cheveyo. "Have you heard from Magnus lately?"

"A couple of days ago he had a question about the area. Why?"

"Suza just called. She's picking up some dark energy that's affecting a large part of the population of Strasford. If it were anyone but Suza, I'd think she was paranoid. Since she accurately senses feelings, I have to investigate."

"I've been through the town a few times but never sensed anything off. Let me know what you find." Cheveyo paused. "And will you be seeing Suza?"

Pope's chest tightened at the thought. "I will, but as my brother."

"Can't you change your appearance back to your old one? It's been six months since Yurek killed you."

Yurek had been assigned to bring Pope back to the other dimension for a death sentence. Unfortunately he'd also discovered Cheveyo and Petra.

Pope shook his head. "I can't chance it. If Yurek sees me, the false memories you implanted of him killing us will be for naught. It's possible that there are other Callorians in the area who could recognize me as well. If they figure out I didn't die, they'll know you and Petra didn't either, and someone will come after us again." He would do nothing to endanger the only family he now had. "Besides, Pope and Suza can never be, for obvious reasons."

"Yeah, getting involved with ordinary humans can be tricky. Petra's fine with me turning into a jaguar, but I'm guessing most women would have a slight problem with that."

"You're being sarcastic," Pope said with a nod. "*Slight* problem." He was trying to master the way humans used language, but it was only 'slightly' easier than figuring out emotions. "As Suza would have in finding out I come from another dimension and that my human façade covers a body 'slightly' different from hers." Not in form, as he still had all the basic components. But his body's composition was beautifully opaque. "Imagine how difficult it would be to explain that I changed my façade."

That he had grown out his brown hair wasn't a big deal, but he was not as tall. Both his facial structure and body mass was different. This time he opted for a look that blended in better, though women often gave him admiring looks—and feelings. The only woman who had captured his fascination was Suza. He felt something that was likely grief at the hopelessness of the situation. "I must go now, as she's in a tense situation. However, I will need to 'port to you and borrow your phone, as my brother cannot have the same number as I."

"Sure—"

Pope stood in Petra and Cheveyo's kitchen, his hand over his eyes. "Is it safe to look?" Once he'd come in without warning and found them in a most interesting position. He'd learned quickly to alert them before popping in.

"I'm alone. Petra's with Amy, getting ready for the baby shower." Cheveyo handed him the phone. "Which you're going to miss, by the way."

"Tell Amy I'm sorry, but I will see her soon. Here, use my phone."

He focused on Suza, her sunny energy that outshined the heartache she'd suffered in life. Her black hair with bangs that framed eyes the color of a storm-tossed night. The memory he visited often of her posed in her leopard underpretties. It stirred him in places he had never felt a stirring in.

In the next instant, he stood behind her truck. If he 'ported to an unknown location, he activated his visual shield in case anyone happened to be watching. People wandered along the street off of which Suza had parked. He walked around the back of the building that housed many shops and then dropped his shield.

He always felt a measure of relief when he successfully 'ported. When he'd been court-martialed for not revealing the information his government knew he was concealing—the existence of the Offspring—he was psychically handcuffed, his abilities stripped. They were slowly coming back but weren't reliable.

An odd buzzing energy thrummed through his being. Something was definitely wrong here. His body strained to run forward, put Suza in his sights. He called the number he had memorized, wanting to call it many more times than he allowed himself. "Suza, this is Cassius. Please tell me where you are."

"You're here already?"

"I drove very fast."

She gave him the street, and he hung up. He would question Suza and then send her back to Flag while he investigated. He didn't see her inside the truck, which worried him. She was a tall woman; surely her head would exceed the height of the headrest. He came up on the driver's side and found her slouched in her seat nervously twisting the silver and turquoise rings she wore on her long, elegant fingers. The sight of her, safe and beautiful, filled his chest with a most strange sensation.

She jerked around to face him, then rolled down her window a few inches. "And you are?"

Smart woman. He had to hide his smile. "Cassius."

She glanced at her oversized silver watch. "Damn, you *were* nearby." The odd coincidence she knew that to be was clear on her expression.

She stepped out, in a tight beige shirt that molded to the 'great mounds of joy,' as Cheveyo had jokingly referred to them. The top hinted at her cleavage, clinging to her long torso, with fringe at the waist. He pulled his attention up before he strayed farther down her tight jeans.

"Nice to meet you." He could feel her disappointment.

She took his outstretched hand, squeezing it firmly. She had the hands of a woman who used them, not rough but calloused. "Same here. You and Pope don't look a smidgen alike." She leaned close, studying his eyes. "Except for the center of your eyes. You've got that freaky-cool violet color, too." She glanced down where Pope was still holding her hand and tugged hers free. "Did Pope tell you what's been going on?"

"A bit. Walk with me and fill me in."

She'd told him most of it, but he wanted to hear it again. As she talked, he watched her, taking in her hand movements, the jingle of her silver bracelets, the grace of her fingers. He figured her to be in her early thirties, more by her world-weariness than anything physical. Her skin was light, though her dark straight hair hinted of her Native American heritage.

"Why are you looking at me like that?' she asked, jarring him out of his observation. "You think I'm crazy, don't you?"

"No. You're right about something being off here. I was imagining what you must have gone through, watching your friend rob a bank."

She was clearly used to people being skeptical of her, or perhaps her gift. Of course, he of all people believed in the ability to pick up others' feelings.

Her defensive posture relaxed. "It was horrible. Carlene has the same evil energy the other people around here do."

"So it appeared that your friend and the other two robbers were working with this man. Or perhaps he had control over them."

She snapped her fingers. "Exactly! You hit the nail on the head."

"With a hammer," he added, that being one of the phrases with which he was familiar.

They had reached the area of town where a crowd watched the police as they interviewed witnesses. Many of the spectators did have blank gazes, while others seemed to be spoiling for a fight, nudging their neighbors out of the way behind the crime scene tape. And they harbored that dark energy he too had sensed in Magnus, though it wasn't as strong. The emotions he did pick up were warped, like a song out of tune.

He turned to Suza, taken aback again by her beauty, even as her expression bore her concern. "Tell me about the man your friend gave the money to. Did he have the same dark energy?"

"You really do believe me." Surprise lit her face. "No, he had the sort of buzzing energy I sense in Cheveyo. Pope. And you."

Callorian energy.

She tilted her head. "Can I ask what it is you and Pope do?"

"You may."

She seemed to wait for more, then asked, "What do you do, and why were you here in town?"

"I cannot answer that. It's confidential."

She blew out a breath, and he sensed what he thought was frustration, something he had perceived in Petra more than once. "You said I could ask!"

"Of course you may ask."

She just stared at him, as though he were an odd specimen. "Poland must be a strange world."

"It is, indeed." Being from Poland was his answer to explain why he didn't understand American nuances. Other things were harder to explain.

She started to say something else but her eyes widened as something behind him caught her attention. “That’s him!” she whispered.

Pope turned his head slightly so he wasn’t obvious. The blond man looked familiar; someone involved in the government in his dimension. Copeland, he thought his name was. He was observing from a distance while he talked on the phone.

Pope leaned closer to Suza, inhaling the scent of perfume and her own scent. “I need you to get closer to him, see if you can hear his conversation.”

“*Me*? Why me? That guy gives me the willies.”

He couldn’t tell her that though Copeland wouldn’t recognize him, he would know he was Callorian by his vibration. “His name is Copeland, and he’s an enemy. There is a chance he will recognize me. He has no reason to harm you. Just be subtle in your eavesdropping.”

“Subtle, I’m not,” she murmured but shored her shoulders and did an admirable job of pretending to window shop as she moved closer.

Humans here were preoccupied with each other’s rear ends, which they referred to as asses. Pope found that odd because asses were also donkeys as well as a derogatory term. He’d understood none of it until he watched Suza’s ass sway with her gait. That it was clad in tight, faded denim only accented her curves. Despite the many hits on her self-esteem, she held herself with confidence.

He forced his gaze to Copeland. The conversation seemed tense. Then he looked at the phone’s screen before returning to the call. He assessed Suza and then dismissed her. Pope soon saw why; she’d affected the same blank look as those who were infected. Amazing woman.

She wandered past Copeland, down two more storefronts, and came back again. He headed down the length of the store and around the corner.

"Nicely done," Pope said when she returned.

"Maybe I'll become a spy. Any job openings in whatever organization you and Pope work for?"

"None, sorry." *Nice try.*

She swiped at her bangs. "I didn't hear any of the first convo other than him saying, 'I have to go. Torus is calling.'"

He'd just figured out what 'convo' meant when the name struck him. "Torus? You're sure?"

"Yes, like the bull. He told Torus the natives were getting restless, that there had been a robbery, though he failed to mention he was behind it. They talked about the earthquake tremors getting more frequent, which is something my friend told me. He said, 'Fine, I'll meet him here in an hour and a half. Is there some reason you have to check for yourself? Don't you trust me?' Then his face got all serious at whatever the person on the other end said, and he ended the call."

Pope rubbed his mouth as he considered what this meant. Torus was part of a team dispatched here years ago, ostensibly to study the energy. The Callorian government hadn't revealed to the general public that their energy cache, buried deep in the ground, was dwindling.

What he did know was that this was bigger than a bank robbery. "Thank you for your help. I suggest you return to Flag and stay away from here for the time being. I will apprise you of the status—"

"Uh uh. There will be no *apprising*."

He raised an eyebrow, something he'd seen the guys do when their women spoke words counter to their directives. Which was often. "Pardon?"

"My friend is caught up in whatever's going on here. I'm the one who called you—well Pope, but still, the only reason you're here is because of me. You're not shutting me out."

Pope moved closer to her, bending his head so that his mouth was close to her ear. "Things are going to get very dangerous."

Her warm breath washed over his jaw when she said, "Are you talking terrorism?"

"Yes. I know Pope cares a great deal about you. He would not want you to be exposed to danger."

"If Pope cared that much, he'd have come here himself. He would have come to visit in the six months since we met. As it stands, we are phone buddies and nothing else, which entitles him to no opinion when it comes to my life."

Pope recognized the hurt feelings. Petra had felt the same when she didn't know Cheveyo's dangerous work was what kept him out of her life. Pope had hoped keeping a connection via phone would be a nice compromise. It wasn't, not for him and obviously not for her either.

"So we need to be back here in an hour and a half," she continued.

"I cannot involve you in this, Suza. It's beyond anything you can comprehend."

She paused, tilting her head. "You said my name the way Pope does. He draws out the 'u'. I suppose you got it from him."

"Did you not hear what else I said?"

She patted his shoulder, the feeling rocketing through him. "I suggest we grab a bite while we can. I'll bet the restaurants have lots of empty tables now. Let's just not go to The Purple Fox. I have no desire for tofu nuggets."

She waltzed off, leaving him to follow. Which was exactly what he did.

# CHAPTER 9

"You're an idiot."

Both Magnus and Erica paused in their futile attempts to break out of their cuffs at Lanna's harsh statement coming through the vent.

"What happened?"

Not Copeland's voice. Erica stiffened. Nester, the brother. She saw flashes of him in her mind, holding Graham's heart, then looking at her. *More*. She shuddered.

"You were zapped," Lanna said. "Probably by the woman who was with the man whose heart you ripped out. I would have let you die, but your brother insisted on saving you. Well, guess what? Copeland orchestrated the robberies without us. Which just shows him that he doesn't need us. So we miss out because of your damned addiction to Darkness, and he's going to rub his competence in our faces."

Erica and Magnus exchanged glances, and she could see the same thought crossing his face: Lanna hadn't mentioned that the woman was in their basement.

Nester said, "Why didn't he wait? He knew I'd wake before long."

"We've got one week to accumulate as much money as we can and hightail it out of Arizona before what's in that tunnel blows this whole area to kingdom come. There are too many things that can go wrong, including the others finding out what we're up to and forcing us back to Surfacia. Think about having to go back to that world where we're so controlled we can't even express emotion. Even Copeland, who can't stand humanity here, hates the rigidness over there. And who knows what kind of punishment they'd slap us with. You have to stay away from that leak, because it's making you crazy. Reckless. When it's all over, you can go your own way and rip out people's hearts all you want."

Erica's mouth dropped open. The cold bitch was giving him permission!

A phone rang, but the conversation was too muted to hear.

Magnus leaned closer and whispered, "It's a lot more than bank robberies."

Erica nodded, the implications astounding. There were others, more than just these three. There would be a massive explosion, and people would die. Not to mention Nester's future victims. "We can't let that happen."

"I'm glad to see that something's given you the resolve to fight."

She rattled her cuff. "Hope's a tenuous thing when you're helpless."

Magnus, still leaning very close to her, seemed to take note of the emotion that had leaked into her words. "Is that something you know well?"

She turned away, searching the basement. "That door over there." She nodded toward a steel door with a lock that made her think of a submarine. "Maybe that goes to the tunnel she mentioned." Her eyes widened. "That means it's *under us*."

"On the upside, we probably won't be alive by then."

"Now who's sounding hopeless?" But he was right. Because Nester was up there, and soon he would be down here. She was sure of that.

Lanna said, "Copeland said the town's in chaos in the aftermath."

"And I missed it," Nester said with a little boy's whine.

"He's on his way back with the money, but he has to go back to town. While he was on the phone with me, Torus called. He's sending Yurek to see what's happening here. Which means Torus doesn't trust us to report back."

Nester's laugh was gravelly and raw. "As well he shouldn't."

"This is all your fault. They probably heard about the 'Heart Ripper'. They're getting suspicious because you can't control yourself. You're going to blow everything for us."

"If you held Darkness, Lanna, you would understand needing the intoxicating power of the energy inside you."

Erica looked at Magnus, who shook his head. "It's an energy, yes, but not like that, at least for me. He's drawing it in directly."

She heard a sniffing noise, then Nester's voice: "Someone's here. Someone with Darkness."

"No, no one's—"

Footsteps pounded across the wooden floor that served as their ceiling, and their voices faded. A minute later, the door at the top of the stairs opened. Nester flew down the steps. His nostrils flared as he took them in.

He pointed at her. "She's the one who zapped me." He turned to Lanna. "Why didn't you tell me?"

"I don't want you to go nuts."

He swung back to Magnus. "But the Darkness is his." He frowned. "He wasn't with her. I would have sensed him."

Nester slammed against the bars, his fingers curling around them. If it weren't for the crazy light in his eyes, Erica might have thought him ordinary, a goofy guy with a too-large mouth and bushy eyebrows. She knew better.

"You put them in my cage. How nice." He ran his tongue up the bar. "I want her. I'm going to take her, and while she climaxes I'll rip out her heart. Doesn't that sound romantic?" That he directed to Erica, and fear washed through her at the thought of either one. Nester leered at Lanna. "Do they do that in those books you read?"

She sounded so droll when she said, "No, generally both parties are alive after the climax. It's more fun that way."

Nester didn't seem to care about the conventions of erotic romance. His brown eyes pierced Erica's. "You shot me. You're one of us."

"Not exactly," Lanna said, stepping up beside him. "They both carry Callorian essence. As Torus found out recently, some of our people did the naughty with the humans here and produced offspring. I believe these two are the result of that."

Nester took them in, his hand flexing. "Two of them. Interesting."

"*He's* mine."

"Yours? Does Copeland know about this?"

"Hands off. I'm sure you can have her, but wait until he returns."

Magnus stiffened at those words even more than at Lanna's earlier assertion. He *was* protective, probably an innate thing.

Nester chuckled. "Maybe you do understand needing the intoxicating energy of something. For you, it's lust."

A door closed upstairs. Lanna snapped to attention, and for a moment Erica actually felt sorry for her. She was obviously dominated and abused by her husband.

"Nester found our guests!" Lanna called up the stairs. "We're down in the basement."

There was some shuffling, and Erica hoped they didn't realize how clearly sounds traveled through the vent. Hadn't Nester noticed when he was kept down here or was he too mad with Darkness?

Suddenly the whole place shook, sending her stumbling and making the cuff pull tight against her wrist. Lanna and Nester grabbed onto the bars to keep from falling. Magnus pushed against the wall, his hands flat to steady him. The shaking went on for twenty seconds.

"They're getting worse," Lanna said as Copeland came down the stairs. "Lasting longer. The Darkness here is growing worse. Isn't it?"

"Torus said the instruments are showing that it's growing at a faster pace. They're having a meeting tonight."

Lanna asked, "Could you feel the difference in town?"

"Yes, Darkness is definitely getting stronger." Copeland gave her a sterile smile. "However, it worked perfectly today. Everyone did exactly as I told them. But people are getting more volatile and, thus, more apt to break free from my control. I don't think we'll get in many more robberies before they start killing each other."

Erica traded looks with Magnus. Explosions, tremors, Darkness getting worse, and people breaking free. What in the hell was going on here? He was taking all this in with terrified curiosity too, if his expression was any indicator. All she knew was that people were going to die, and she couldn't do a thing about it. Taking out killers had given her purpose, a sense of control over a world with damned little of it. Now she was back to square one.

Lanna's expression grew panicked. "Will Yurek come here?"

"If he does, we have to eliminate these two before he arrives. Their presence would raise questions about how they came to be here that we don't want to answer." Copeland shot Nester an irritated look. "If I call you, take them into the tunnel and shoot them. Do it near the second escape hatch so you can stash their bodies in the storage cabinet. While I don't plan for Yurek to come down into the basement, I'd rather only have to come up with an explanation for the cage and not why the walls are splattered with blood. So no heart rending."

Lanna took Copeland's hand, giving him a coy smile. "I have a proposition for you. I've been a good girl, you have to admit. *I* haven't gone off the edge." She shot Nester a look before reviving her sweet smile for her husband. "I have done everything you've asked, while you have done nothing that I've requested. But if you give me this one little thing, I promise I won't bother you for a year."

"The human male is not a little thing."

"No, he's not." Lanna bit her lip. "It's only for the next seven days, and then we'll be out of here, and they'll be dust."

Nester's laugh had a cackling quality to it. "Everything will be dust!"

Lanna rolled her eyes but kept her attention on Copeland. "I won't break your touching rule, because I'm going to…" She whispered the rest in his ear.

Copeland considered. "All right, have your fun. But you cannot release him." He looked at Nester. "No killing the woman yet."

Erica's heart jumped. She wasn't sure if that was a good thing or not.

"Whaaa?" Nester's face scrunched up. "She gets to play with them and I don't?"

"You've been a bad boy, Nester. You will accompany me into town and you will behave."

And like a little boy, Nester stomped up the stairs, his shoulders hunched. Lanna clasped her hands together and kissed Copeland's cheek. He shrank away from her, as though repulsed by the act.

Lanna seemed used to the rebuff. “Thank you.” Hands still together, she turned to Erica and Magnus with a huge smile.

# CHAPTER 10

Pope returned from the restroom where he'd tried to 'port to Magnus. He could not, and the block he encountered was disturbing. Nor could he reach him via phone. He returned to the table just as the server delivered their food.

"Real meat," Suza said as she eyed the burger in its sesame-seed covered bun.

He was uncomfortable about her being involved, but he was familiar with this particular combination of stubbornness and drive to protect someone. Those in the grip of it would not be swayed. All he could do was keep her out of danger until she realized she was in over her head. Which would be soon.

Society in Surfacia was highly ordered. People obeyed. Here, they followed their emotions. Feelings were new to him. Picking up Petra's and Cheveyo's feelings had woken his own. That he had never experienced them made each one unnerving. And some, tantalizing.

"Tell me about Pope." Suza picked at her cheeseburger with mayo, lettuce, pickles, and other messy things that dripped down her fingers as she ate, requiring her to run her tongue down those fingers and…

He blinked, completely thrown by the sensation in the pit of his stomach and an area that's function was, well, merely functional.

She stared at him in a way that made him think he had a bug crawling down his nose. "I'm not asking you to spill any secrets," she added, clearly perplexed by him.

A good reminder that she would look at him that way many times if he tried to have a relationship with her.

"Pope is…eccentric. No sense of humor, none at all."

"Are you kidding? He's hilarious. I haven't had a man crack me up like that in years. Granted, he doesn't mean to be funny, but he seems to enjoy making me laugh and he never takes it personally." She let out a soft sigh. "I love that about him."

Her smile was so warm and radiant, he got caught up in it for a moment. He shook his head. "And he is quite naïve when it comes to relationships."

She waved that off, then stuck her pointer finger in her mouth to suck off the mayonnaise. "I got that. It's cute. The guys I've dated, well, they're all plenty experienced and they think they're God's gifts to women, know what I mean? Like I should be *grateful* that they're paying attention to little ole me." She shook her head, making her bangs swish across her forehead.

"But you are beautiful and personable. They should be grateful for *your* attention."

"Bless you." She tilted her head. "See, that's the kind of thing Pope does, throws out these compliments without meaning to, which means he means them." She rolled her blue eyes. "He gets me all tangled up."

He had heard plenty about how she had suffered the consequences of not trusting her psychic feelings warning that her boyfriends were loathsome pigs. He could listen to Suza's stories in person forever, watching her animated face, the deep pink lips she pursed frequently, the pert little nose she wrinkled. All he could do was drink everything in before he had to leave her again. For good, he was afraid. Maintaining their connection was difficult for both of them. Petra teased him, saying that he was in love with her, that he pined for her. He was not sure how one could feel a tree for someone, but he did know that he felt deeply cut whenever he hung up. Felt it now at the thought of ending their friendship.

"Cassius?"

He realized she'd been saying his phony name for some time now.

"I was saying, tell Pope he makes me feel good in a way that is so genuine, so real, it breaks my heart not to see him again. But if he can't be in my life, it's probably best not to continue our conversations."

Pope couldn't breathe for a moment. Finally he said, "That is a wise ultimatum. My brother is not a good man for you, Suza. Trust me on this."

She set the remainder of her sandwich down. "Give me one good reason."

A smacking noise drew their attention to a table nearby. The man and woman seated across from each other were bracing their hands on plates of food to keep their balance as they kissed ravenously.

Two men were arguing at a corner table over who paid the bill last time.

"This town has gone crazy," Suza whispered.

Suddenly the whole place started shaking. Glasses slid off tables, silverware clattered, and anyone who was standing grabbed for something to steady them. It lasted a full thirty seconds before abating.

"They're getting longer," someone said in an agitated voice. "This whole town's going to crack apart."

Pope glanced at his watch. "I must go."

"We must go." Suza reached for her purse, but he waved it back and put a large bill on the table.

He did not want her involved with these people. He knew them; they disdained humans and had no issues terminating them. It struck him that he was now in that same category. Making it all the more dangerous for her to be with him.

They headed down the sidewalk, which was still quite busy with what Petra called lookee loos and journalists getting interviews for their stories. He headed to the place where Copeland had spoken to Torus. Pope would have to be very careful to keep his distance so neither sensed his vibration.

He was keeping his eye on the scene when he picked up on that very vibration. Subtly he turned to find…Yurek. The shock of seeing the man assigned to terminate him was bad enough; that he was walking right toward them was inconceivable. The man's gray eyes were always bland and emotionless, so Pope couldn't tell if he'd recognized his vibration.

Pope didn't think; he acted. He grabbed Suza and pushed her into a store's alcove as though he could not wait another moment to plant his mouth on hers. His arms went around her, snug around her waist. The feel of their mouths mashed together knocked all sense from him. She made a squeaking sound, her hands slapping against his chest but remaining there. Her fingers tightened on his shirt, and her lips softened for a moment before she pushed him back.

"Cassius!"

Pope had to pull his thoughts together enough to surreptitiously glance in Yurek's direction. He'd continued on, but that didn't guarantee he hadn't picked up on something. Agents of the government in particular maintained a calm façade at all times. Which was why Pope was having a hard time reconciling the way his heart was pounding.

"I apologize," he said, trying to remember the reason for his rash behavior.

"W-what was *that*?" She put her fingers to her mouth.

"It was rash behavior."

"Well, yeah, I got that. I like your brother, you know." She narrowed her eyes at him in a speculative way that made him nervous. "You don't look much like him, but you feel like him. Like you have a good heart, but that doesn't make sense, because a man with a good heart wouldn't kiss the woman his brother's been flirting with on the phone."

"There is something about you, too, that makes a logical man act in illogical ways." He glanced in Yurek's direction, spotting him meeting up with Copeland. "But I did have a tactical reason for kissing you. The man over there might also recognize me. I needed to hide my face in a manner that wouldn't raise his suspicions."

The two men walked around the corner and out of sight.

She tugged her shirt down. "Well, I'm glad to hear that. I'd hate to think I misread you."

She had read him too well.

"You stay here. I'll go around back."

Pope wished he could hear them. He wished Suza would stay put. Neither was going to happen.

She followed right behind him. "Should I wander over again?" she whispered.

"No, it's too risky for you to do that again. But since you insist on accompanying me, you must help me appear inconspicuous. As we have already been spotted in a lip-lock, it would not be unusual for us to have ducked into the alley to continue our mad passions."

She raised an eyebrow at him. "If this weren't so serious I'd swear you were just trying to make out with me."

"I am not, and we should not engage in the actual act of kissing. It's distracting, and I must try to listen to their conversation. We will merely—I think the correct term would be cozy up—over there, against the wall."

"All right." She shook her finger at him. "But it's only an act."

He wrapped his arms around her waist. She laced her arms over his shoulders, which pulled her flush against his body. He willed his penis not to react, focusing instead on the two men who would kill him instantly if they knew he was there.

He buried his face in the crook of her shoulder, inhaling the faint scent of her perfume. Her fingers tightened on him, and she let out a soft gasp when he moved up the side of her neck. Her silver feather earring tickled his nose.

"Don't go any higher," she whispered. "That's my spot, just under my ear."

"Your 'spot'?"

"My *spot*. The place that drives me crazy."

He stilled his movements, shifting so that he could keep an eye on the two men who were deep in conversation. They walked closer as they talked. He had to push past the feeling of Suza in his arms, her warmth and scents and the amazing newness of it, and concentrate on his hearing.

"Why haven't you told Torus how bad it's gotten here?" Yurek asked.

"I just discovered how fast the volatile behavior has escalated in the last few days."

"Be ready to depart at a moment's notice." Yurek glanced their way.

Pope didn't hide his face, knowing that would look suspicious. But he pulled Suza close and kissed her because that's what a man who was in an embrace like this, in an alley like this, would do. All the while he kept an eye on the two men who had continued on and were moving away. They gave each other the slight bow Callorians used for greeting and departing and headed their separate ways. Pope rolled what he heard around in his mind. Whatever was going on here was escalating fast. That was obvious by the erratic and wanton behavior of those in town. Their base emotions,

Suza had said. Yes, he could understand how easily, with some influence, one could give into those desires.

"Cassius? They're gone."

He pulled back, clearing his throat. "Yes, they are."

Suza appeared to be dazed but blinked to clear it from her eyes. "And they have something to do with this weirdness."

The *whoop* of a siren pierced the air from the direction of Main Street. Someone on a loudspeaker ordered the crowd to disperse, and people began filtering into the alleys. Laying his hand on Suza's shoulder, Pope pulled her close as blank-faced people passed by. She didn't object, her fearful gaze taking them in.

What did the Callorians have that was making people into zombies?

Pope picked up a Callorian vibration right before a man behind him asked, "Do I know you?"

Pope turned to see Yurek wearing a suspicious expression. Pope held back his instinct to attack. It was in Suza's best interest to bluff Yurek and get rid of him. "I've recently been sent to check on things. My name is Cassius."

Yurek flicked a glance at Suza, but his steely gaze returned to Pope. "I'm Yurek, also recently assigned here." He held out his hand.

Pope eyed it. Yurek had no interest in participating in this dimension's custom. He wanted to sense Pope's energy. Could Pope pull it off? He clasped his hand briefly and released it just as fast. "I'm sure we will see each other again."

Yurek's voice lowered. "Yes, we will." Then his face morphed into Pope's former visage, tall with a shaved head and violet eyes. "It *is* you, Pope," Yurek growled, staring at his reflection in a window before turning back to Pope. "I sensed your energy but thought it couldn't possibly be because I killed you. But here you are." His puzzlement changed to rage.

Suza let out a startled gurgle. "Pope? But how…*killed*?"

Beyond the bizarreness of seeing his former visage was the fact that using their powers in public was forbidden. Pope pushed Suza out of the way and knocked Yurek's hand from where it was about to touch his neck. Yurek had physically connected with him, which meant he could now mimic Pope's abilities the same way he could mimic his looks. Odd that he'd picked up Pope's default visage and not his current one.

"Suza, leave," Pope managed as he used his outstretched hand to use his Flare before Yurek could do the same. Yurek flew backward, sliding across the asphalt, but he managed to send a Flare at Pope. He couldn't dodge it because Suza was right behind him. So he grabbed her and threw them both to the ground.

He rolled them so he was facing Yurek, who was on his feet and stalking toward them. He had gone back to his normal visage and was rubbing his palm where the Flare had initiated. "Your powers are weak. But somehow you managed to implant false memories. That's why there were no bodies to bring back. So the hunter and his girl are alive, too, I imagine. I will remedy that as soon as I kill you."

Pope pulled Suza to her feet and pushed her away. "Go." Out of the corner of his eye he saw her run. She was no fool, thank goodness. The thought of her being hurt…

Yurek called out to the people who had paused to watch the show. "Grab her! And bring her back to me."

To Pope's horror, they did as Yurek bid and ran after her. Suza had obviously heard Yurek because she picked up her pace. One man in the small mob was faster, tackling her. Pope sent a low-dose Flare at the people who fought her efforts to break free. It worked like a force field to knock them away from her.

Yurek took advantage of his diverted attention and slammed into his back, sending him to the ground. Claws sliced toward his neck, and he turned to find Cheveyo's black jaguar leaning down to finish him off. Once Yurek had absorbed another's ability, as he had with Cheveyo, he kept it, talented son of a bitch.

Pope thrust his hand out, pushing away the jaguar's jaw. Its hot breath moistened his fingers, the tips of its teeth grazing his skin. Where was Suza? He heard the struggle continuing, with her screaming, "Bastards, let me go!" Pope summoned his power, feeling his palm heat. No, he still hadn't recovered his full power, but he had enough to throw the panther several yards where it hit the back of the building with a satisfying *thwump!*

He lurched to his feet and spun to Suza where, incredibly, the mob had obeyed her. They stood in a confused state, staring at their hands.

Yurek commanded, "Grab her and do not listen to anyone but me! Get both of them!"

The zombie'd people moved forward again, eager to do Yurek's bidding if the bloodlust in their eyes was any indication. Pope used his low-dose Flare again to shove them back as she dodged others who were trying to keep her from escaping. Seeing another group of people approaching, she ran back to Pope's side. He could grab her hand and 'port away, but what if it didn't work properly, and he left her there alone? Its reliability was still shaky. He would stay and fight.

"God, one's a kid. A kid!" Suza said, moving up beside Pope as they watched the people gain their feet and advance again. Their bodies were scraped and bleeding. Suza held out her hand. "Stop!"

This time they didn't obey her. They advanced with the single-mindedness of movie zombies but a lot faster.

Pope turned to find Yurek leaping toward them in panther form. Pope grabbed Suza's hand and 'ported to her truck. He'd had to take the chance. She spun around with a gasp.

"Suza, get in the truck. We need to leave now."

She opened her mouth to ask what was probably a thousand questions but clamped it shut and jumped into the truck. Once they were locked inside the cab, she patted her shoulder. "I don't have my purse!" She ducked down beneath the dash and groped around before extracting a key, which she jammed into the engine starter. Within minutes she was driving down the side street, slowed by clusters of people wandering aimlessly. Her fingers clutched the wheel, and her face was frozen in fear and determination.

"Suza—"

"Don't talk to me!" Hysteria edged her voice. "Not while I'm driving, 'cause I'm going to go friggin' nuts and then I'm going to go insane and bonkers right after that, and I'm trying not to do any of those while I'm driving a five thousand pound vehicle."

"Don't 'nuts', 'insane', and 'bonkers' have the same meaning? Of course, 'nuts' can apply to other things, too."

She shot him a look—and feelings—he didn't know how to interpret, which was probably just as well. They were soon out of the business district, such as it was, and heading down a road with a smattering of businesses. She drove into the parking lot of a pet store that was permanently closed, stopped the engine, and jumped out of the cab. Her blue eyes were wide as she paced, fingers tunneling through her hair and leaving it mussed.

As soon as he came around the front of the truck, she stalked toward him. Within a foot of him, she stopped, fear and confusion in her eyes. "What the hell just happened? Who are you? Who was that man who *changed* into Pope? Where is Pope?"

"Please, you must calm down."

She laughed, the kind of sound that could shatter glass. "Calm down? Seriously? After what I just saw, what I went through, you suggest I calm down. Oh, that's priceless."

He wanted to touch her, at least put his hands on her shoulders, but that didn't seem wise at the moment. "I need to return to downtown and follow Yurek, the man who attacked us. But I cannot leave you in this state where you might go nuts, insane and bonkers all at once."

"He called you Pope, and then he turned *into* Pope." Her eyebrows furrowed, half hidden by her bangs, as she studied him. "He said he killed you, or thought he killed you. This sounds so crazy coming out of my mouth, but…you're Pope, aren't you?"

He decided that confirming that would be more beneficial than denying it. "Yes. When we met you the day you were in your underpretties, we were in the middle of a battle with Yurek."

"My underpretties?"

"What I call your under garments, which were very pretty on you."

For a moment she smiled, then shook her head. "So when we met, this guy was after you?"

"Yes. That is why Cheveyo sent you away for a while, to keep you safe from any fallout. Yurek was sent to terminate me, and if we'd killed him, my government would only send another in his place. So we implanted a fake memory in Yurek's mind of him killing me, Cheveyo, and Petra, the woman who was with us. I had to change my looks in case he ever saw me."

She searched his face. "You had plastic surgery?"

"In a manner of speaking."

"But how did he turn into you?"

"He has an ability, a supernatural ability you'd call it, to mimic the look of those he touches. Somehow he picked up my former visage."

"And he, he turned into a friggin' panther!"

"Technically, it's a jaguar. That is Cheveyo's ability, to become jaguar. But for good, never evil."

"Cheveyo's like you?"

"Sort of."

She rubbed her forehead, obviously trying to assimilate everything. "Why is this man hunting you?"

"I'm an outlaw. A Scarlett. Once I was the highest-ranked officer in my government's police force. But then I had to make a choice: lose my position or expose humans here who are like my family to certain death. I chose to save them."

She took his hand, turning it palm up. He bore no mark, no indication of his power. "You threw those people back with some kind of force. You tossed that horrible man several yards."

Pope couldn't help but smile at the relief that surged through him. "My powers are definitely returning. I haven't had to use them in the last few months, so I have not been working with them." He also liked the way she was touching the center of his palm, searching for whatever produced the Flare.

Her gaze slowly lifted to his, her eyelashes fringing eyes filled with question. "What are you?"

"Suza, you can drive home and forget everything you saw. Including me. You will be safe and sane, and I will do what I can to find out what is going on here and free these people. I suggest that you do."

She had not released his hand. "I sensed that you were different, you, Cheveyo, and Petra. I still feel your heart, Pope. I could never forget you, just like I couldn't forget what just happened. Whatever is going on here, I'm involved. Because of my friend. Because of that kid who's being used by them. And because of you. What are you? Tell me."

She looked calm enough to handle it, but he wasn't sure she *should* handle it. Perhaps if she knew the truth, she would run screaming into the hills.

"I'm a form of human from a parallel dimension, as are the two men we were watching. Because our kind lived deep within the earth, near the magnetic field, our energy and physicality changed, as did our abilities. We lost the density of the human form. Our energy vibration runs higher, so we can change our form or use that energy in different ways. We use what you call the sixth sense with ease and regularity."

"Parallel dimension? Really?"

"Your scientists, the smart ones, have already figured out that there are other dimensions besides this one."

She sat on that for a moment. "What is your dimension like?"

"Much like this one, physically. But it is run more strictly. We are not allowed to express our emotions because our government believes they are the downfall of mankind. I suspect that what is affecting the people in Strasford is something called Darkness. It's an accumulation of the repressed emotions of our people. Many years ago it became a large energy field that men tapped into to gain darker powers. Two men did that and then came through a portal not far from here. I think Darkness may have come through, too. Obviously my people have learned they can use it to control the humans here."

Suza swayed, her pupils so wide her eyes appeared nearly black. He lunged forward and caught her around the waist. She looked as though she was about to pass out from overload.

"I have you," he said. And she felt good in his arms in a way that nothing else had.

She put her hands on his upper arms. "I've never fainted before," she murmured, looking into his eyes. She smiled, her eyes still dazed. "You kissed me. Pope kissed me."

He chuckled. Her mind was definitely overloaded if that's what she focused on. "I've been wanting to do that ever since you put your hand on my chest and said I had a good heart."

"Kiss me again."

"Pardon?"

She gave him a stern look. "I think you heard me."

"But did you hear me? You know what I am, what I'm involved in. And you still want to kiss me?" He felt an odd buzzing in his chest.

She nodded, then leaned up and kissed him, putting her hand to his jaw. Her mouth opened to his, lips soft and warm against his. Her tongue touched his, running along the length of it, and the buzzing grew louder. He mirrored her movements, momentarily losing himself in the sensations bombarding him.

She finished the kiss and backed up. Her eyes were clear again. "I knew you were different." She shook her head in an exaggerated way. "I never imagined quite *how* different. I'm not sure I understand everything you told me, but I do know something horrible is happening that's affecting a lot of people. And I know that whatever you are, you are a good man. Take me, Pope."

He blinked, taken aback by her command. "Here? Now?"

She laughed, full and robust. "I mean, take me with you. I want to stop these people."

A mix of relief, joy, and fear mingled in his chest. He nodded. "Let's go back to town and find Yurek. He is no doubt looking for me."

They spotted him before he saw them. Suza remained several car lengths back as Yurek drove through town searching. At the end of his pass through the main street, he continued on, heading toward Las Vegas.

She peppered him with questions and took each answer in. “Will Yurek tell the others about you?”

“It is doubtful. That would mean admitting he’d failed, and our government doesn’t tolerate failure. He will try to kill me without the others knowing.”

Midway to Vegas, Pope and Suza looked at each other.

“Did you feel that, too?” she asked.

He nodded. “The energy got lighter, like we reached the outer edge of Darkness.”

She turned back, her expression troubled—and determined. “We have to stop this, Pope.”

“There’s too much at stake to fail.”

# CHAPTER 11

Lanna returned not long after they heard the door close upstairs. She'd changed into a tight sweater that accented her cleavage and small waist. She had a nice figure, Magnus would give her that. But her icy blue eyes, pale complexion, and white-blond hair reflected the lack of warmth in her soul. She reeked of the same desperation he'd seen many a time, and that was bloody unattractive. Still, he had to pretend she was all that if they had any hope of getting out of there.

She visually checked their restraints before unlocking the cell door. Holstered on her hip was a knife. Once inside, she relocked the door. That would be problematic, though he was sure he could wrangle the key unless she tossed it outside the cell.

One step at a time.

She prowled closer, taking him in as though he were some specimen. He wondered if this was how some women felt when a guy leered at them.

"Some of the people with us have Darkness, too," Lanna said, nodding toward the tunnel door.

He arched an eyebrow. "You have others locked away in the tunnel?"

"No, they're part of the group who…they're near Vegas. So far they haven't come in through that door." But the possibility worried her, by the crease of her forehead. She seemed to push that thought away. "I haven't seen any of the Darkened ones over there Become, but I've heard they're dangerous." She raised her hand toward him, hesitating only an inch from his face. Probably remembering that her husband would know if she touched him. "Are you dangerous, Magnus?"

He played into her game, trying not to let his focus stray to Erica. "Very. But only to the wrong people."

"What animal do you Become? Nester used to be something resembling a bear, but since he's been sniffing Darkness, it's warped him into some grotesque creature."

"I'm a mountain lion. Sleek, fast, with fangs and claws. Too bad I can't show you."

She made a *tsking* sound. "No, you can't. If it were up to me, I'd release you and screw your brains out." She traced her finger down her throat.

"It is up to you. We're alone, aren't we?"

She chuckled. "You just want me to let you go so you can haul ass."

"Can you blame me? Your husband's going to kill me. I don't particularly like that idea. Maybe I can take you with me." Erica stiffened, but he kept his heated gaze on Lanna. "Your husband obviously doesn't appreciate you."

Something changed in Lanna's expression, a raw and oh-so human need. "I couldn't," she blurted out, but the idea clearly intrigued her. "I just want to experience passion."

"And what do I get out of pleasuring you?" Besides the chance to escape. Her need for fantasy might cloud her judgment, but she was no fool. She'd be suspicious if he were too willing. "A guy likes sex wherever he can snag it, sure, but it's a bit difficult to conjure the mood when you have a hatchet hanging over your neck."

Lanna flicked a glance to Erica. "I won't let Nester kill her. I know you're protective, that it's your nature. And she's terrified of dying the way her companion did. I can save her that."

"Deal."

He had to keep in mind that Lanna could sense emotions. He didn't need any special ability to see that his cooperation pleased her. She came closer and took out the keys he wanted so badly. He stilled his own enthusiasm at the thought that she was releasing him. His arm fell to his side, prickling as the blood returned to it. The cuff was still tight around his wrist, curbing his abilities.

She drank in the sight of him. The woman was starved for sex, no doubt about it. And from the way her fingers flexed, she wanted to touch him so bad that she ached. She visibly forced herself back and, surprisingly, approached Erica, who regarded her with suspicion. Erica's eyes widened, she gasped, and then her pupils dilated. Lanna released her cuff from the bar, though again it was still around her wrist. Erica wasn't in there anymore. For the first time, he saw no fear, want, or suspicion on her pretty face. It was eerily blank.

"What did you do to her?" he asked, his chest tight.

Erica straightened and walked toward Magnus. "I'm in her head, controlling her." Erica's voice sounded different, and then it hit him, that she was *in* Erica. "I haven't used this ability in years. I can't use it with my own people, and I'm not allowed to use it on the regular humans." Erica's smile was stiff. "But now it will come in handy. I can experience everything without violating Copeland's stupid rule."

He didn't like it, even if he had touched Erica. And deep in her blue eyes he saw stark terror. She stumbled toward him, her body falling against his. Lanna laughed through Erica. "I am so out of practice." She remained against him, her hands sliding over his shoulders, hips grinding against his pelvis.

Suddenly her fingers gripped him so hard that her nails jabbed into him, and an unholy scream tore from Erica's mouth. He saw her in there, trying to take control as she grabbed her head and thrashed her body so violently that she knocked Lanna to the floor.

Lanna scrambled to her feet, knife ready. She opened the cell door, ran out, and closed it behind her. She was stunned, but Erica was still freaking out, muttering, "No, no, no, not again!"

He reached out and grabbed her hand, pulling her closer. "Erica! It's all right."

Except it wasn't because they'd probably blown their chance to use Lanna's lust to escape. She'd run up the stairs, obviously shaken, but right now all he cared about was Erica.

She blinked, coming back to herself. Her face was pale, and tears streaked down her cheeks. "She got into my head. *Controlled* me."

This vulnerable side of the tough woman reached out and grabbed his heart. He tugged her against him, using his free hand to stroke her back. "It's done. She's gone."

He kept stroking and whispering inane words meant to calm until she stopped shaking and whimpering. Her hand rested against his chest, and her fingers flexed and contracted involuntarily.

"I can't imagine how freaky it was to have someone inside your head," he said trying to understand her reaction. He knew her brother Jerryl had gotten into one of the Offspring's heads and tried to force him to kill his friends. Eric Aruda had fought the bastard's directive and shot himself to save them.

She pulled back, wiping her hand across her eyes. He didn't release his hold on her though, letting his hand slide to her shoulder.

The words she'd screamed came back to him. "You said not again.'"

She shook her head. But it hit him then, the man he'd just been thinking about who could get into people's heads. *Her brother*.

"Jerryl got into your head?"

She wrapped her arms around herself, and in her eyes he saw shame and pain and anger all twisted together. "I'm not talking about this with you."

He couldn't resist needing to figure it out. Figure her out. "Have you talked to anyone about it?"

She kept her gaze averted. "No one who believed me."

"I believe you."

She shuddered at those words, and he could see her struggle. "Why do you care?"

"I don't know, but I do."

She still stared at a spot a couple of feet to the right of him. "I couldn't push him out. I wasn't strong enough when he…"

"When he…" He didn't want to hear this, but he needed to. For some reason, he needed to know the shadows this woman harbored. He had a feeling they were even darker than what he held.

"He made me do things to him," she whispered. "Sexual things. And I couldn't fight him. I was a kid. I didn't have any power then."

Magnus's hand tightened on her. "Sick son of a bitch." He held back the violence that boiled inside him at the thought.

"He said it was okay because we had different fathers. I'm not sure how he knew that, or if it was even true."

He stroked his thumb over her shoulder, his stomach turning. "Who did you tell?"

"Jerryl threatened to kill me if I did, but finally I went to my father. He suggested I was just jealous, because Jerryl was so good at everything and got all the attention, that I was making this up in an ugly attempt to get some for myself. My stepmother didn't believe me either, since she always sided with my father. They thought Jerryl was a hero. He'd saved a boy from drowning when he was eight, pulled him from a lake. I was into trouble a lot, wasn't doing well at school. Early on, he would control my mind and make me do things like tear my clothes off and run screaming through the house. Of course they thought I was mentally disturbed, so my allegations fit that diagnosis. All Jerryl's plan, I'm sure."

Magnus raged for her, for that girl he was imagining. "Your life must have been hell."

"I left at sixteen, stayed with some people who let me work at their store to earn my keep. I was okay then."

But she wasn't okay. Now her shields made sense, as did her need for human connection. When she reached out though, she had no idea what to do, especially with her shields up. If only he'd known, but it wasn't like she would tell some guy she'd met in a bar. Aye, maybe he was a drummer psychologist.

She swiped at her face. "Why are you being so nice? I probably ruined your chance to escape."

"*You're* free."

She seemed to just realize she was no longer cuffed to the bar. She took a step back, and he had to force himself to let her go. She held out her hand but still couldn't produce a glow.

He let his arm remain aloft. "And my hand is free. It's a start."

She studied him, as though she wasn't sure what to make of him. "You're not like anyone I've ever met."

"I could say the same."

She went to the cell door and tried it. "I'll bet." She turned to face him, her eyes red and wet. Somehow it was beautiful on her. "Why are you looking at me like that?"

"I'm glad you told me."

She shrugged, but her cheeks reddened. "What does it matter? We're going to die here anyway."

"We don't have to."

He nodded to the vent in warning, and she came close again. He wished he could pull her closer but that was probably pushing it. He did put his mouth to her ear, letting his jaw brush hers. "We've got three people to deal with: cold, crazy, and horny. We need to play their dynamics to our advantage. Lanna is our best hope. She's got a weakness we can exploit. And she doesn't have a deadly ability."

"How can you be sure?"

"Copeland told her to shoot us if that guy comes here. Why would she need a gun—or knife—if she can blast us?"

Erica nodded. "True."

"If I can make her believe that I'd take her away from two men she obviously doesn't like, she'll release me. But I have to convince her I want her."

"But that means I have to let her into my head."

"I don't like that part either, but it's the only way she can live this fantasy of hers. And it weakens her."

"No, I can't. I can't go through that again. It's too much like Jerryl, making me do things…"

He lifted her chin to make her look at him. "But I'm not Jerryl, and I won't do anything you don't want. Let the heat of it sweep her away. Before she goes too far, I'll tell her I can't touch the body of an unwilling woman. While we're discussing it, you knock her to the floor and nick her keys. Once I'm out of these cuffs, I can Become." She still looked terrified. "You know you can kick her out."

"That's because I took her off guard. Next time she'll be ready to fight me."

"If there's some other way, I'll try it. Any ideas?"

She studied the cell, chewing her bottom lip. After a minute, she shook her head. "I can't come up with anything else."

He ran his fingers down her arm, circling her wrist gently. He felt the raised scars. She was a fighter. And potentially someone who had wielded her power to kill. "Do you want to survive?"

She glanced at the tunnel door. "I want to stop whatever's going to happen." She would do it to save others.

He turned her hand so that her palm faced up. She bore a scar there, too, of her power. "You're not afraid to die?"

She shook her head.

"You're not afraid to kill either."

She shook her head again without hesitation.

A weird combination of fear and pride twined through him. "Was that why you were following me? To kill me?"

"Only if you were the Heart Ripper."

"You thought I was the serial killer?" He almost laughed at that.

She, however, looked dead serious. "Because you said there was something wrong with you. Then you went to the park where two of the victims were found."

"Two of the victims? Are you investigating the murders?"

"I was hunting the killer."

"Hunting…"

Confidence and pride shone in her eyes. "I hunt killers." She flexed her hand. "And I kill them. Eight of them so far. I almost got Nester."

"Holy hell." He'd thought she was this vulnerable woman, and here she was killing killers.

"It makes me feel like my life here has purpose. That everything I went through made me strong enough to stop murderers."

He could hardly wrap his mind around her.

She kept that fierce expression when she said, "I suppose if I'm strong enough to do that, I can do what you suggested." The ferocity melted away as she looked into his eyes. "Can I trust you?"

His heart broke for the fear in her eyes at the prospect of trusting anyone but herself. Of being let down again. "With every cell in your body."

# CHAPTER 12

It took about an hour before Suza stopped staring at Pope. Sometimes he glanced her way, but he didn't seem to mind her gawking.

"My great, great grandfather was a shaman," she said. "There were rumors that he spoke to aliens out in the desert. I've always believed there's life on other planets. Maybe those 'planets' are actually other dimensions."

"There's something you *haven't* told me about your life?" He gave her a smile that told her he didn't mind all the chattering she'd done over the phone. "I'm amazed."

She gave him a coy smile. "There are a few things you don't know about me."

His long fingers tightened over the top of the steering wheel. "Until this trip, I didn't know about the sensitive spot beneath your ear."

She recalled the feel of his mouth on her neck, when she thought he was the inappropriate brother. "I have a lot of sensitive spots. I don't want to tell you about them." She fought to keep a straight face at the disappointment on his face. "I'd rather show you."

"Oh." His cheeks actually reddened. "*Oh.*"

"Later," she added with a smile as the full impact of what she'd insinuated seemed to sink in. "Do you have any sensitive spots?"

"I don't know."

"What do you mean, you don't know? Everybody has at least one of *those* spots. Beyond the obvious ones, of course."

"In our dimension, intercourse is for a purpose, such as physical release or procreation. Sex does not sell, and we are not preoccupied by the attributes of naked bodies. We are taught that those here are obsessed with such things, that their sexual desire corrupts them, causes them to act in immoral and illegal ways. That we are lucky not to have those desires."

His gaze drew down her body. "But we are not lucky. We are deprived, though I never felt that way until I met you. The sight of you posed on the couch in your underpretties has been a preoccupation ever since. It is a new thing for me, desire, wanting to kiss a woman, and do more than kiss a woman."

"When you say 'new,' do you mean…new?" She flattened her hand on her chest.

"Desire is yet another emotion we have been bred to repress and deny. But I cannot deny it with you. The people in my life cannot bear to be apart from the object of their desire, but it goes deeper. The thought of that person being hurt causes them physical pain. They go to extraordinary and dangerous lengths to save one another. I did not understand this until you." He reached for her hand, thoughtfully lacing his fingers with hers. "It's baffling and disturbing and wonderful all at once."

She looked at those strong, sexy, and capable hands, and then into those mysterious eyes. "You're saying you've never desired a woman before me?"

"I'm afraid all of this is quite new to me. Other than textbook learning. I understand, for instance, that sex is inserting the man's penis into the woman's vagina, but I don't know what elements transcend the act into 'making love.' I do know there is a great difference. If we continue interacting, you would have to teach me, well, everything. You would need to show me what actions pleasure you, and I would have to practice over and over to get it right." He took her in, completely serious! "It's troublesome. I can see by your expression and by…I'm not sure what your feelings indicate."

She threw herself against him and kissed him.

He tried to keep an eye on the road, and Yurek's car, but still managed to participate in the kiss. When she sat back, he said, "That is not a troublesome prospect then?"

She laughed, the only way to release the bubbles of joy building in her chest. "You've never been in love with a woman before? Or had sex with a woman?"

He was clearly perplexed by her reaction, but then again, she had trouble getting her head around it, and *she* was feeling it!

"No, but I do have curiously strong feelings about you that might fall into the 'in love' part. Having nothing to compare, I suppose it will take time to figure out what they are. You may have to teach me about emotions as well, as I barely have a handle on the array of them. My friends find it exasperating to explain what I feel from them."

"What you *feel* from them? Now you're sounding like me."

"Yes, I too pick up human emotions, experiencing them in the same way they are. But I don't always understand them, so I ask what they mean. I want to learn."

"I'll have to explain what I'm feeling?"

"The subtle ones. If you're upset or hurting, it helps me to understand, so I can make things right. I understand the basic ones, but there are many that perplex me. Like yours right now, for instance. You're exuding an odd mixture of surprise, elation, and other emotions I've never sensed before. Curiously, none are frustration."

"Oh, no, darlin', I'm not experiencing frustration. I'm wrapping my mind around this. You. So you'll want to know what I'm feeling, so you can help me feel happy all the time?" She stifled a sigh. "And I get to teach you everything about making love, being loved?"

"I will need thorough instruction, yes. The parts work fine. I have experienced the physical manifestation of desire with you a few times already."

She thought she might already love this man, who was not a man, which made him all the better.

He gestured to his gorgeous body. "I want to use this to pleasure you in many ways."

A small mewling sound she'd never made before came out of her mouth. A man who listened to her, really listened, and would take learning how to pleasure her as seriously as he took his former job as an officer. A man who probably couldn't lie or deceive to cover his emotions. Holy schmoly.

"I'm in." She took his hand and kissed each finger, and then turned it over to tickle his palm with her tongue. "I'm so in."

He growled low in his throat. "As eager as I am to start our lessons, now is not the time. Yurek's turning off the main road," he said, his voice still strained. "We should probably—"

"Yes, you're right." She released his hand. "We can talk about this later."

"I see why the Offspring males were so adamant about not falling in love during a mission. This is all very distracting."

She was eager to meet his sort-of family who all had psychic abilities.

Pope passed the road where Yurek had turned, and the sign that read, *CAL ENERGY RESEARCH CO.* Beyond that, another sign warned that trespassers would be prosecuted. "These people will kill me once they find out who I am. I'm afraid they would kill you, too, if given the chance. You have already seen that. We must keep our concentration sharp."

The thought of him being killed—hell, of either of them dying—shot adrenaline into her veins. "Then that's what we do."

"This never worked with the women I've known, but I must give it a try. You should stay in the car and be safe."

"And leave you to figure this out for yourself? No way."

He released a long breath. "I suspected that would be your answer."

He pulled down the next road and followed it to an abandoned factory. He got out and surveyed the hills in the east. "There's a finestra somewhere around here."

She joined him. "A what?"

"A portal that allows us to travel back and forth. I was never privy to what this group was doing here and had forgotten about them until now. Given what's going on in Strasford, and their obvious connection to it, I have to conclude that they are manipulating Darkness for ill intent."

"Yeah, what you said."

"The only way to find out what they're doing is to go in." He lifted his hand. "I may have to kill one or more of them if we're caught."

He had told her about his powers and how they were coming back. She pulled her .45 caliber Springfield out of the glove box. "I don't have anything as wild as you do." She tapped the side of the gun against her palm. "But I can blast someone the thoroughly human way."

His mouth twitched ever so slightly. "Have you shot anyone?"

"Shot *at* my ex once, when I caught him trying to steal my truck. I missed him 'cause I didn't want to hit my truck. Hearing this baby go off did the trick though. He scampered like a little girl with her panties on fire. I have a practice range in my back yard. I'm not a bad shot."

She swore she saw a glint of pride in his eyes. "I imagine. Do you have binoculars in here as well?"

"I do." She dug them out.

He surveyed the surrounding area. "I want to go up there where we will have a better vantage point."

She followed his pointing finger to a spot high up on the side of the hill in the distance. "I don't even see a road—"

He put his arm around her, and suddenly they were at the spot he'd pointed to.

She blinked, swaying on her feet. "Even though I know you can do that 'porting thing, I wish you'd give me some warning."

"I did." And he was serious.

She patted herself, making sure she was in one piece. "Okay, *more* warning. Like, 'I'm about to whoosh you to a whole new location in a blink of an eye'."

"I will keep that in mind. If I have time. It seems to be working now, though there's a chance it will fizzle out. What worries me more is only being able to 'port myself, leaving you behind. That possibility frightens me, because these people have skills like mine. Even with your gun skills, you will have little chance of surviving." He let those words sink in for a moment. "That frightens you."

"I'm scared, yes. Scared of a lot of things right now, to be honest." Not the least of which was falling for a dude who wasn't quite human. "But being scared has never kept me from doing anything. Sometimes to my detriment, yeah, but knowing what's at stake, there's no way I'm backing down."

He nodded, then lifted the binoculars to his eyes and studied the community below. A few moments later, he handed her the glasses.

She saw a large building off to the side, some smaller ones, and a neighborhood on the other side. "Reminds me of an old mining town."

"See the small building off to the side? A lot of people are coming out."

"Could they all be crammed into that small shed?" She glanced at her watch. "It's five o'clock. Quitting time."

He placed his hand over hers. "I'm going to take us down, to the back of that building."

"Thank you for the warning." After another stomach-tumbling moment, they were standing behind the building. She could hear people talking, both men and women, though it wasn't easy to hear what they were saying.

The blast of a horn nearly shot her up in the air two feet. They'd been spotted!

"Attention. Attention," a man's droll voice came across loudspeakers all around the area. "There will be a meeting in the main hall at seven o'clock. Attendance is mandatory. Our deadline is being moved up. Repeat: our deadline has been moved up."

That had nothing to do with their presence. But it was probably connected with that Yurek character discovering how bad things were in Strasford.

She and Pope held each other's gazes as they waited for the sounds of people to subside. He wrapped his fingers around her wrists and nodded toward the building.

*Here we go again.*

The building housed not much beyond an elevator. She and Pope both spun around, ready to encounter someone. She lowered her gun but kept it at her side as she followed him to an elevator.

Pope pressed his finger to his mouth—like she would start chattering *now*—and approached it. A dizzying moment later, they were standing outside that same elevator, though the damp air indicated they were probably several stories down. Behind them a tunnel stretched interminably under the glow of green lights. He kept his hand on hers as they headed into the unknown. Her boot heels echoed on the stone floor. She removed them, tucking them to the side in a patch of shadow, and continued on. The floor was smooth and cool.

After thirty minutes, they stopped to investigate what looked like an escape hatch, with a ladder that led up into a narrow, dark opening. Nearby was a locked cabinet. They continued on, hearing an occasional *drip-drip* and finding a place where some underground spring was leaking down the wall. None of it was as bad as the sense of claustrophobia gripping her.

Pope sniffed the air, slowing his pace. He raised his hand, and a glow emanated from his palm, enough to illuminate the dirt wall. He took several more steps, clearly on the trail of something. Then he found it, only she didn't know what *it* was exactly, other than a white, rectangular box. Beneath it was one of the bright orange paint marks they'd been seeing every so many feet. This, however, was the first such box they'd come across.

Pope walked farther, coming upon another such device above the orange mark. He leaned close to her ear and whispered, "Explosives from my dimension."

Explosives. In a tunnel. A tunnel they were deep within. *Let the panic breathing begin.*

He put his arms around her shoulders and pulled her close. "Calm down."

She nodded, big jerky movements.

Soft footsteps echoed down the tunnel, coming from the direction in which they were headed. *Oh, great, throw that at me right now.*

Pope pulled her back to the hatch they'd passed, pointing up the steel ladder. She went first into the hole of pitch darkness. He followed close behind until they were above the roof of the tunnel.

The footsteps grew louder, then a man passed below them. Everything would have been just fine if he'd continued on. But he didn't. He paused, stepped back, and clicked on a very large flashlight. Which he began to point up at them.

Pope dropped on him, sending them both crashing to the floor. The flashlight rolled across the ground. Suza pulled the gun from her waistband—and stopped. *Explosives. Tunnel. Gun a bad idea.*

Pope twisted the man's arm behind his back in a way that looked painful. "What are you doing here? I'm an Elgin for the Callorian government and demand an answer."

"If you were an Elgin who was dispatched here, you'd already know what was going on." The man unleashed a wave of some kind of energy blast that threw Pope against the wall. "And you wouldn't bring a *human* down here." He thrust his hand toward Pope.

Pope's hand was already out, the glow flashing bright on his palm. A beam of light shot out and seemed to surround the man, whose face contorted with pain. He gritted his teeth as he tried to summon his own power, but the glow grew brighter and brighter, and he went *poof!* A shower of sparks rained down onto the floor and then there was nothing left of him.

Pope looked eerily calm. “I didn’t want to take a chance of igniting the explosives, but I had no choice.” He stared at his palm. “It took a lot more effort than it used to.” Which meant he could normally kill people with much less effort. *Won’t Mom be so pleased?* He dropped his hand. “Let’s go.”

He took her by the elbow and guided her onward, as though he were leading her into the Dang Ranch Bar for a night of dancing. She was trapped in a tunnel deep belowground wired up in explosives with a man who clearly was used to killing. Now she knew what being ear-deep in trouble really meant.

As they continued, so did those white boxes, every few yards. With every one that they passed, the word *kaboom!* popped into her head.

Pope pulled her to a halt as a sound echoed up ahead.

# CHAPTER 13

Magnus had predicted that Lanna would return as soon as she'd gotten over being ousted. Calling her down would seem desperate and might pique her suspicion. Once Erica had made up her mind to let the vile woman in, she wanted it over with. She wanted out of there before Nester came back.

Magnus gestured for her to come closer. Now that she was free to move about the cell, for what that was worth, she could move up very close to Magnus. Only to communicate quietly, of course.

"Remember that she can pick up feelings," he whispered, his warm breath washing over her ear and neck. "It's fine to feel afraid; she'll expect that. We don't want her to pick up on hope."

Hope, that shaky bitch. "Or our plans. I don't know if Jerryl could pick up my thoughts when he was in my head."

"Bastard," Magnus muttered. "It's a good thing he's dead." His fingers clenched. "Or I'd kill him myself."

The girl inside her cried out in release that he would avenge her. The woman she was now wanted to throw her arms around those broad shoulders and bury her face against his chest. Even when he'd been a stranger, there was something about him that tugged at her to let go. He had held and comforted her as she'd spilled the horrible secret that haunted her soul. She had seen no pity or anything to indicate he saw her as damaged.

"You alright?" he asked. He lifted his hand, the cuff jangling, and touched her cheek. "Of course you're not, dumb question." His voice was soft and low and washed over her. "If this works, we run together, agreed? No splitting off."

"I'm going there." She nodded toward the tunnel door, which made his fingers brush against her cheek. "To figure out what they're doing. Then I'm finding one of the escape hatches they mentioned."

He moved his thumb across her soft skin. "I know you're used to being on your own. Bloody hell, taking on killers by yourself." He shook his head. "But for now, we're together."

She shivered at the words. "Okay."

They heard the phone ring through the vent but couldn't hear any of the conversation. What they did hear was her raised voice in some other part of the house. Something displeased her.

Erica turned to Magnus. "Uh oh. Sounds like the guy is coming here. She has to kill us now."

He stiffened. "If she does, we have the opportunity to overcome her in the tunnel."

The door opened, and Lanna padded down the stairs. Her face looked flushed, but she took a deep breath and visibly composed herself as she reached the bottom. "We have to leave town sooner than expected. So if we are going to have our time together, we have to do so now. The good news is that Copeland and Nester will be in town longer. They have to, um, sort out our finances."

Erica released the breath that had tightened her chest at the thought of dying immediately. But what did it mean that they were leaving sooner than planned? Was the terrible thing also going to happen sooner?

"Lanna, Erica has agreed not to fight you if you want to try again. She understands the value of not having Nester kill her. Seeing her friend die like that was traumatic."

"And having someone mind control me was freaky, too," Erica added.

Lanna stepped up to the bars. "I was shocked that you could push me out." She eyed Erica's cuff, probably making sure it was still on.

Erica assumed her victim persona. "I just wigged out. I didn't know what I was doing."

"Mmm," was Lanna's reply, as though she weren't quite sure. "You I can handle leaving loose like that." She turned to Magnus. "You are much more dangerous."

Magnus jangled the cuff still attached to the wall. "I'm only dangerous when I'm threatened or if someone I care about is. What I didn't tell your husband was the fight I jumped into was over a woman I was seeing. Two men were trying to hurt Jessie, and I stepped in to protect her. One tried to kill me, and I guess one healed me.

"I was in a coma for a few days, and when I woke, Jessie and my brother had fallen in love. I love my brother, but I wanted to rip his head off. That's not like me, especially since I was only infatuated with Jessie. It has to be the effect of Darkness." He raked her with a heated gaze. "I can't imagine how it would be if I was really in love. I've never loved a woman, but now I would consume her, possess her, and kill anyone who hurt her." His eyes started to shift toward Erica, but he trained them on Lanna.

Erica watched him work his magic. That's what Lanna wanted, a dark, dangerous, sexy man who would protect her, obsess over her. And Magnus was all of those. He was also compassionate and honorable. Erica knew he was telling the truth about Jessie, sating her curiosity about the woman.

Erica sensed Lanna's intrusion now that she was prepared for it. Like a vine growing into her psyche, it snaked its way in, numbing her deep inside. Everything in Erica wanted to fight, to oust her. Panic gripped her, the invasion bringing back those times of losing control of her body. She breathed through it, keeping her focus on Magnus. He gave her strength with his steady gaze.

*You're in control of at least being out of control. This is your choice.*

Lanna unlocked the cell and stepped inside, relocking it as usual. Erica took note of where she tucked her keys. Lanna walked over to Magnus, breathing in the scent of him with her eyes closed. "Possess me." The intensity of that statement swept through Erica, and her body stepped forward. "Consume me."

There was only one thing that would save Erica's sanity—focus on Magnus. She had been intimate with him, after all, and she was attracted to him. Her hands went to his chest, pressing against his pecs, and Lanna's elation rushed through her. Erica focused on her thumbs circling the smooth skin around his nipples and making them harden.

When Jerryl took over, she was horrifyingly aware of everything. She locked her soul in a box deep inside her for protection. In the years afterward, the box became her safe haven. She climbed into it when she went after a murderer. And when she had sex.

*That's why you never feel anything.*

That something Magnus picked up was her soul's need for connection, for touch. And, oddly, she *had* felt a link to Magnus. Still felt it, even under Lanna's control. She let herself out of the box a little more, connecting to what she was doing.

His skin was smooth and soft, a contrast to the hard planes of his body. She leaned up on her tiptoes and kissed him. He had initiated their kisses. Now her mouth opened against his, and she plunged her tongue in. His hand skimmed her shoulder, not violating the boundaries he had set. He gave her a soft squeeze, a secret signal: *I know it's you in there.* She signaled back, a gentle pinch at the back of his neck. She loved the way his curls wrapped around her fingers, silky soft.

The sound of pleasure that came out of Erica's mouth, she wasn't sure it had come from Lanna. In fact, most of her recent actions weren't Lanna driven at all. But Lanna hadn't seemed to notice, perhaps too caught up in everything. Which was exactly what they wanted, Lanna completely immersed in the sensations she so longed for. Fantasized about. He would give Erica a cue to oust and overcome her at the right moment.

The irony was not lost on her that a woman uncomfortable with sensual pleasure now had to indulge in it to save her life. She drew her hands down

Magnus's sides to his waist, hooking her fingers on his belt loops and pulling him against her. His mouth hungrily devoured hers as he ground into her. His body was cooperating nicely.

"Eri—Lanna," he murmured, catching himself in the nick of time.

He'd started to say her name. She pushed the thought from her mind before Lanna picked up on it, or precisely, the way it made her feel.

"Magnus," Lanna said on a breath behind her. "Oh, yes." She directed Erica to run her hands over the front of his jeans.

He was fully erect, thick and hard, and Lanna sighed. "Just like I imagined. Copeland's got a penis the size of a pencil. I want to feel you, Magnus."

Erica's mouth drew a wet line down the center of his stomach. Her fingers started to unsnap his jeans. Magnus slid his hands over the top of Erica's head, his fingers tunneling through her hair. The signal.

Erica's heart pounded as she readied to throw her out. This had to go perfectly. *One. Two. Three!*

She pushed Lanna out and shoved her backward. They both fell to the floor when Lanna grabbed onto her. Something hit her hard in the cheek, and the cuff clicked onto the bar.

Lanna stumbled to her feet, breathing hard and backing away from Erica.

"I'm sorry," Erica said, saying it to Magnus for not succeeding but looking at Lanna. "I freaked again. Do you know what it's like to have someone inside your head making you do *things* to a man you don't even know?" She kept babbling, hoping Lanna didn't think the move was calculated. "I'll try it again and this time I'll hold on."

Lanna was visibly shaken, scrubbing her hand back through her short hair. "No." She shook her head and looked at Magnus. "It was amazing, but you were right: it's a tease going through someone else. And the thing is, I want to do more than just touch you. I want you inside me, and I can't experience that with you shackled to the wall. It won't work." She turned toward the door, clearly overwrought.

"What if we left together?"

Magnus's words stilled her, and she spun to face him. "What do you mean?"

"No offense, but your husband is an arse. He mistreats you. Dismisses your needs and desires, and in fact derides them. He neglects you. And when he hit you, I wanted to kill him."

Something rippled across her face with every word he spoke. "You did?"

"You're not the bad guy, he is. You're innocent, so I have no ill will toward you. You're in a bad situation. Obviously there's going to be some explosion, and you're going to run." He gave her a soft smile that tightened Erica's chest. "So run with me."

Lanna's chest rose with the deep breath she took. "I…I don't know. Copeland would kill me if I ran off with you."

"He'll have to find us first. And I know the perfect place to hide, far from here."

"You wouldn't just run off after we left? Leave me?"

"You know what I am, what I harbor. That if I fall in love with you, I will possess you. Consume you. If you're willing to be with me anyway, why would I leave? You're beautiful and sexy and the only woman who understands what I am. And I know what you are. We wouldn't have to hide our true natures. Including that we both enjoy sex. A lot. We're a perfect match."

He was good, so good Erica felt a tremor of fear that he was serious. That he'd leave her.

*Can I trust you?* she'd asked him earlier.

*With every cell in your body.*

Lanna's face lit up. "We *would* make the perfect couple." She stepped closer, her hand hovering inches from his bare chest. "I could touch you all I want, and read all the sexy books I wanted, too."

His voice was low and seductive when he said, "You could read me the best parts, and we'd act them out. I would spank you until your ass was pink and tender, and then I'd kiss away the pain."

She sighed, closing her eyes and pressing her mouth to his chest. Her hands came up, gripping his sides. "Yes, yes, yes. I want that."

"The sooner we get out of here, the more time we have to put distance between us and your husband."

"I'll take the money. I know where he's probably hidden it."

"Don't give him another reason to hunt you down. If you, Erica, and I are gone, he'll be pissed, but he probably won't bother taking the time and trouble to chase us down."

"You're right." She pulled the keys out of her pocket. "And he'll be even less likely if I leave her." She nodded toward Erica. "There won't be two of you out there to trouble him."

Fear gripped Erica's heart. Magnus had inadvertently given Lanna a good reason to leave her behind. Lanna unlocked his ankles first, giving Magnus a chance to meet Erica's gaze. He kept his expression blank, giving her the slightest nod.

Lanna was watching him as the second cuff opened. She sprang up and reached for the final cuff around his wrist. Erica couldn't breathe as the key turned in the hole and the cuff snapped open.

Magnus groaned as he pulled his arm down and rubbed his hand.

Lanna turned to Erica. "I'm sorry I can't keep my promise. Then again you didn't live up to your end of the deal eith—"

Magnus grabbed Lanna's arm and snapped the cuff around her wrist.

"Sorry that I won't be able to run off with you." He grabbed the keys where they'd fallen and released Erica. "You had me until you were willing to leave Erica here to face the wrath of your husband."

Erica could barely breathe with how fast everything had changed.

Lanna shook her hand. "What about me? You're leaving me to his wrath!"

"Yeah, I'm sorry about that, too." And he did look sorry. "But I can't take a chance that you'll alert him or the others."

Lanna screamed every expletive as Magnus unlocked the cell, then relocked it behind them. They ran for the door, and Magnus turned the round wheel to open it. The door screeched as it opened, then clanged shut behind them.

Erica felt the same way she did when the roller coaster took its first plunge, her stomach shooting up to her throat.

Lights led down a long tunnel that went both ways. Oblong white boxes were mounted along the walls but didn't seem to be lights.

Magnus drew them closer to one of the boxes and patted the surface. "They said that what was in this tunnel was going to blow the area to kingdom come. It doesn't look like anything."

She drifted a few feet in the other direction. "They go this way, too, at least as far as I can see. But something feels weird here."

He felt it, too. "Not Darkness. This isn't heavy like that. It's vibrating right through my body."

She backed up, bumping into him. "Let's go in the other direction."

He gave her no argument. "Whatever these boxes are, they were installed recently. The lights are dusty, and the boxes are clean."

"I don't like it. Someone has calculated the distance between them. See the orange marks?" She pointed to the florescent marks at floor level.

"If they're explosives, they'd act like dominoes, each one setting off the next."

She trembled at the thought of being in the tunnel when that happened. "And the timeline's been moved up. How do we stop this?"

"We find one of those escape hatches and alert the authorities. We can't do this on our own."

They came across a metal ladder attached to the wall that went up into what looked like a dark hole. Magnus climbed up, and she heard his grunts of effort.

"I can't see a damned thing," he said from some distance up. "Nothing I feel turns or opens." He came back down. "Let's keep going. We'll try every one we come across. One's bound to open."

They had a little time before Copeland and Nester returned, but once they did, they'd come after them. And so would a very pissed-off Lanna. Twenty minutes passed before they came across another metal ladder. Magnus climbed up and had the same kind of luck.

"How long does this tunnel go on for?" she whispered.

"I'm more worried about what's at the other end."

# CHAPTER 14

Nester followed Copeland into the house, stomping his feet.

"Nester, stop acting like a child."

"Stop treating me like one. *I* wanted to pull off the robbery. I missed out on the first ones—"

"That's your fault. If you hadn't been out there snorting Darkness, you would have been part of them."

Copeland didn't understand. Just because he was cold and empty didn't mean everybody was. He treated his beautiful wife like a secondary citizen, and he treated Nester like a child. Nester had never experienced such power and exhilaration as when he fed the Darkness in him with more. Soon it would be gone, blown back to their dimension, so he had to take in as much as he could now.

"Lanna!" Copeland yelled as he headed into the back bedroom with the satchel.

Nester wondered if his brother planned to double cross him, using the excuse that he had been the one to procure the money. He'd given Nester permission to go off and kill as much as he wanted when they split off from the group. As though he were ready to get rid of him. Wouldn't it be nice to be on his own without having to answer to his brother? As long as he had money to survive.

"She's probably down in the basement with her puppets," Nester said, creeping toward the door and listening. He had read some of her books, though he'd never admit it. What the people did in them was interesting. He might like to enact some bondage and torture. "I don't hear anything."

Copeland opened the door. "Lanna, your toys have to go now."

Nester followed, hoping to glimpse something sordid and deliciously erotic. He slammed into Copeland because he'd stopped midway down the stairs.

"What the..." Copeland took the rest of the stairs.

Nester couldn't contain the giggle that erupted. "Well, well, lookee here."

Copeland shot him an irritated look, clearly missing the humor of finding his wife cuffed and the prisoners out of sight.

"Don't even start with me," she said, though Nester could see the fear of Copeland's retribution in her haughty expression.

"Where are they?" Copeland asked, about to turn back toward the stairs. "We have to find them before they report us to the authorities."

"They went into the tunnel," she said.

"The *tunnel*?"

"So you have nothing to worry about," she said.

"Nothing? You stupid bitch, we have even more to worry about if the others find them."

She flinched. "We could run now."

"We run right before we're to report to the finestra, so they don't have time to look for us." Copeland tossed the keys to Nester. "Unlock her and meet me in the tunnel. We have to find them." He opened the door and disappeared in the darkness within.

"Does that mean I can hunt them down?" Nester asked, rubbing his hands together.

"Yes," he called out, his voice echoing.

Nester turned to Lanna. "I think I'll make you wait. You've been a very naughty girl. Tsk tsk." He jammed the keys into his pocket and ran into the tunnel.

In retrospect, going into the tunnel hadn't been the best idea. No doubt Erica was thinking the same as they walked for an hour and a half, trying every escape hatch they came upon to no avail. Having the information they needed was useless if they couldn't tell someone. Returning to the house wasn't an option. Copeland and Nester were probably back and on their way.

Magnus and Erica approached another one of those damned escape hatches, and he wondered if they should even try.

"Thanks for not leaving me there," Erica said in a soft voice.

"Why are you thanking me? Like there was a choice?"

She kept her gaze trained ahead. "I've only known you for a day. You're a phenomenal liar. You could have been lying to me as easily as you were to her." She didn't mince words, this one.

"You're right. You have no idea what kind of man I am. And the truth is, I did leave a woman locked in a cell knowing her husband's going to be angry as hell with her. I don't feel good about that part, but I do what I have to when it comes to my survival. I spent my whole life training to kill a man who was trying to kill my family. Now that I've finally gotten to the point where I can live, my life is once again ripped out of my hands. So I would lie, I would screw a woman, and I'd kill to get that chance. But I'd never leave an innocent woman to die."

"But I'm not innocent."

"Yes, you are."

She wasn't like most of the women he'd been with, fun-loving, light-hearted, out to have a good time. But the two women who had drawn him deeply were troubled, harboring dark, dangerous secrets.

Jessie. He didn't feel the painful tug when he thought of her. He didn't feel exactly that with Erica either, but he did feel something. A tug, aye. Erica would never be a fun-loving toss-in-the-sack. But he needed to make her smile. To fill her big blue eyes with something other than distrust, uncertainty, or the shadows that dwelled there.

"Why are you looking at me like that?" she asked.

"Like what?" He really wanted to know, as he had no idea what expression revealed.

"Like you want to save my soul."

Ah, that one. "It's just that we might die in this tunnel, and I've never made you smile. Or sigh with pleasure."

She did smile, though it was more of a Mona Lisa one. "You did."

"I did? Which one?"

"I'm not telling. You'll get a big head. A big*ger* head."

He threw his head back, stifling his laugh. "My head's not that big, you know. It's the curls."

He sensed it coming up behind them—Darkness. Instinctively, he pushed her behind him as he spun to face it. Through the gloom of the tunnel, a black form raced up at the speed of Darkness. It took him over in response, transforming him into a mountain lion. But not quite fast enough. Nester slammed into him, throwing them both against the wall.

Magnus was ready for the impact, tightening his form and leaping up to attack. He tore his fangs into Nester's shoulder. Lanna was right; Nester wasn't any particular form, just vaguely the shape of an animal. He definitely had the one. Nester growled and snarled and whipped his head back and forth, his fangs more like a saber tooth tiger's.

Magnus stole a glimpse at Erica, who was searching for a weapon. He needed to dispatch Nester before his cohorts arrived. By the footsteps pounding in the distance, they were on their way.

Nester bit Magnus's thigh, tearing away his dark flesh. It hurt, as Jessie's dad had warned, but it was only fatal if his opponent kept tearing bits away before he could mend himself. Magnus would try the strategy on Nester. The thought of Erica, of protecting her, gave him the ferocity of the Tasmanian Devil.

Erica was warming her ability, her palm glowing brighter than her earlier attempt.

"Don't use it unless you have to," Magnus warned.

She wore an expression of worry, obviously hearing the footsteps, too.

Nester ducked away from Magnus to lunge at her. She dodged, but not quickly enough to evade being shoved off balance. Before Nester could try again, Magnus jumped on his back. Nester rammed him into the wall again and again, trying to dislodge him. Magnus drew his claws across Nester's throat, like that bastard had done to him days ago. Of course, Nester wasn't a mere human, so one swipe wasn't going to do it.

The sound of Copeland's labored breathing was louder than his footsteps. The tunnel lights dimly lit his approaching form. Now this was going to get tricky. Nester was enough to fight. Copeland had a weapon as deadly as Erica's, but he had more juice behind it.

Copeland stopped a few yards away, bending over to catch his breath. No sign of Lanna.

"Kill this son of a bitch," Nester said. "I want the woman."

Magnus kept his hold so his brother couldn't Flare him without getting Nester, too. But that left Erica open. As Copeland straightened and flexed his hand, a white light flashed around him. Arcs of lightning shot out, strong enough that electricity prickled across Magnus's skin and lifted the hairs on his arms. Erica held her hand outstretched, her face in a grimace.

A glow emanated from Copeland's palm, but he was crumbling. His knees gave way, sending him to the ground. He arched, his eyes bulging. He wasn't the only one screaming in pain. Magnus tore his gaze from the now seizing man to Erica, who was contorted, eyes squeezed shut and mouth in a grimace. When Copeland collapsed, so did she.

"Erica!" Magnus couldn't go to her without releasing Nester.

Nester was staring at his brother's body in shock. He slipped out of Magnus's grasp and went for Erica's still form.

Magnus headed him off, throwing him several yards where he skidded across the floor. He heard more footsteps running toward them. Lanna? No, from the other direction. Not good. Nester got to his four feet and stared in the direction of the approaching footsteps. Then like a shadow, he tore off toward the house.

Erica was curled in a fetal position and crying in pain. He morphed back to man and dropped down beside her. "Shhh, baby, shhh. Someone's coming."

He scooped her up and threw her over his shoulder. Dead weight. The words felt as heavy as she did. Her ability was killing her. He knew it was painful to use, but she'd never said anything about it debilitating her. Locating the ladder, he took the steps carefully, holding onto her with one hand, the railing with the other. He cleared the tunnel's ceiling, which put them in the shadows, and whispered for her to remain quiet. His arms were trembling from the effort to hold her and hold them in place as well. Especially with her shaking so badly.

Two people ran up right beneath him, and he heard a man whisper, "Back. There's a body."

Erica started whimpering, her breathing shallow. Hell, they were a sitting target up there now that they'd revealed their presence. Magnus held her tight and dropped down, ready to Become. He came face-to-face with Pope and a woman he didn't recognize.

They looked as relieved as Magnus felt. Pope took in Erica, still clutched in Magnus's arms. "She's hurt?"

"Yeah." There wasn't time for explanations. "Can you get us out of here?" He knew the bloke could teletransport. That would come in real handy about now.

"I can try. Anyplace in mind?"

"My motel room would be best."

Pope touched the woman's arm, then put his other hand on Magnus's arm. "Picture the place clearly in your mind."

He experienced an odd flickering feeling, the way the power comes on and off during a storm.

Pope shook his hands, his frustration clear. "My abilities are still unreliable. We've been 'porting a lot since we got here. I tried going to you, but I was blocked by something on your end."

"The cuffs. Never mind," Magnus said at Pope's raised eyebrows. "Try again."

Erica clung to him, digging her fingers into his shoulder. She was burning up, damp where their bodies touched. Pope put his hands on them and this time Magnus felt a *whoosh*. In the next instant, he was standing in his room, his duffel bag on the bed right where he'd left it. He shoved it to the floor and laid Erica down, then climbed up next to her and took her hand. She gripped his hard, which he hoped was a good sign.

Magnus scooted even closer to her, pressing his body against her side. "This is Erica Evrard."

"Jerryl's sister," Pope said.

The name churned his insides. "Yeah."

Pope moved closer, assessing her. "I've had a hard time keeping tabs on her. What happened? I do not see any injury."

"She's got the same—" Magnus stopped, taking in the woman with him. "Talent as you," he finished.

"Suza knows everything." Pope gave her what seemed like an affectionate smile and then turned back to Erica. "She can Flare?"

"Yeah, though she calls it Lightning. Copeland, the guy who had us captive, said her body can't handle it because she's human." Magnus lifted her sleeves to reveal the scars.

With the demeanor of a doctor, Pope pushed the sleeve higher, running his fingers along the lightning-like scars. Then he pulled down the shoulder of her shirt. Newer scars snaked across her skin, red and angry. "It's killing her, quite literally. When I use it, the power of the Flare goes through me, too. But yes, my body can tolerate it. The scars appear to be moving toward her heart, though of course I can't tell without disrobing her. Do you know?"

Hell, he'd slept with her and hadn't seen her naked. "No."

Pope held his hand over her. "I used to be able to heal, but I wasn't able to heal your Darkness. Then again, I'm not sure that's even possible."

"I appreciate everything you did. I may not have been in a state of mind to properly thank you after I woke up."

"You had a lot to process." Pope kept his gaze on his hand as he spoke, but he glanced at Magnus. "You are coping now?"

"As best as can be expected, considering I got kidnapped and was nearly killed by your people. And one with Darkness, too. He's not dead. Yet."

"My people? Seems as though we're involved in the same problem. Now we can work in unison. But first we must get her on her feet again. Do you know how long she suffers like this?"

"We just met. I've never seen her use her power." She killed killers. Magnus held that tidbit in, still amazed by it.

Pope lowered his hand. "I'm not certain I did any good. Suza and I need to return to the Vegas area and move her truck before the others find it. I will 'port us there and try to 'port us back with the truck."

"I heard you did that with my Beemer," Magnus said, finding it hard to imagine.

"Yes, but I hadn't recently used my 'porting ability several times. I barely got us here. If we do not return right away, know we had to drive back. It took approximately an hour and a half to get there. That should give your Erica time to recover. I fear we're going to need all of us because we are facing something rather large."

"And we don't have a lot of time."

Pope seemed surprised that he knew that. "No, we do not."

Suza came up to Pope and wrapped her long fingers over his arm. She was as far from the person Magnus would have paired with Pope as he could imagine, with her oversized silver jewelry and low-cut tank top edged with fringe. She had bare, dirty feet, and they both looked as though they'd done some tangling of their own.

"We'll compare notes when you return," Magnus said. He gave them the highway directions back to the motel.

Once again they flickered, which looked bizarre as hell. It took several tries before they disappeared. Nothing would surprise him anymore. Except for caring about this prickly woman he'd only just met. He gathered her in his arms.

"Don't die on me, Erica," he whispered next to her ear. "I want more chances to make you smile. And sigh."

She tried to crack open her eyes, but they barely focused.

"What can I do?" he asked, holding her face in his hands. "How can I help?"

"Just l-leave me alone. I'll be all right." She moved out of his grasp, curling up and facing away from him. That's what she said. Her thoughts were different.

*Need comfort.*

He spooned up behind her, mindful where he put his hands. "Not this time."

Her body slowly relaxed, and her breathing evened out. Ten minutes later, she rolled over onto her back, and her eyes fluttered open. She seemed confused to find him hovering over her.

"You're in my motel room," he said. "You killed Copeland."

She ran her hands over her arms. "You were fighting Nester."

"He got away. He heard someone coming down the tunnel and took off. Even though he must have figured they were his people, he probably didn't want to have to explain himself. And us."

She looked around, stunned. “More of them came? Are you sure we’re not dead?”

He chuckled. “Aye. I sure hope Heaven isn’t a cheap motel room.”

“But how…”

“The people who were coming down the tunnel are on our side.” He let that sink in for a moment, enjoying her dumbstruck face. “I don’t know the whole story, and since they’re not back yet, I’ll wager we won’t hear it for another hour and a half. The DNA in us that makes us part Callorian came from Pope’s father. Pope is an outlaw as far as his people are concerned, but he’s been an ally to those who carry his DNA. He and a lady I’ve never seen before are here doing the same thing we are: trying to stop this explosion. They went to get her truck, and then they’ll be back.”

Her shirt was still askew over her shoulder, and Magnus brushed his finger over her scarred skin. “He says you can’t keep using your ability, which you likely inherited from him. Your body can’t handle it. It’ll kill you.”

She pulled her shirt up, dislodging his fingers. “I know. It gets worse every time.”

“You’ve been doing this *knowing* it’s killing you?”

She met his eyes, hers filled with both shadow and the light of having purpose. “It’s all I have.” She looked at the bathroom door, which was ajar. “I need a shower.”

“Are you sure you’re okay to do that?”

She rammed her fingers through her mussed hair. “I feel gritty and dirty, so even if I have to crawl in, I’ll do it.”

"I'm in there right behind you." At her startled look, he added, "After you're done and out of there."

He stayed close in case she got dizzy. She was weak, her hand brushing the wall and then holding the door frame, but she didn't wobble. She closed the door and turned on the water. He leaned against the door, listening to make sure she was all right.

A few minutes later, she emerged, wrapped in a towel. "I feel loads better. If only I had clean clothes."

He dug in his duffel bag. "I just threw in some stuff, having no idea how long I'd be away. Here." He handed her a T-shirt, only belatedly realizing what it said on the front.

She raised an eyebrow at the rather suggestive drawing of two drumsticks and the words, *DRUMMERS KNOW HOW TO USE THEIR STICKS.*

He shrugged. "It's just for banging around. I have another one—"

"It's fine."

"Can't help you in the pants department."

"This is good. Having a clean shirt was the most important thing. Go ahead and shower." She raised an eyebrow. "Should I hang out by the door to make sure you're all right, too?"

He started to open his mouth but realized she'd not only noticed but realized why he'd done it. He shrugged. "It's just the way I am."

"I know." There was that smile he wanted to see, even though it was hesitant. Their eyes locked, and his chest tightened. Why did he fall for dangerous, haunted women?

# CHAPTER 15

As soon as the shower started, Erica slipped into the long T-shirt. It was dark blue, so she skipped the bra. The fabric was soft against her skin, and it was freeing to stay in just the shirt, even if only for a short time.

She searched the room. Was Magnus being serious about them just popping in? After what she'd seen, she would put no amount of weirdness past reality.

Some of that weirdness was how she was watching the bathroom door waiting—no, anticipating—him coming out. In the short time she'd known Magnus he'd been flirty, sexy, scary, determined, and protective. He would have been better off leaving with Lanna and saving his own ass.

*It's just the way I am.*

Her breath hitched, but she pushed those wayward thoughts from the edge of her mind. She wandered to the mirror and flicked on the light. She could hear the water hitting Magnus's body, so he was still busy in there. She stripped off the shirt and studied her reflection. Something in her eyes looked different, a light she had never seen before.

She forced her gaze to her upper body. The new scars were red and burned, and they now covered her shoulders. Before today, they had come up to her biceps. Before today, she'd been all right with dying. But now the reality stared her in the face: the electrical shocks were growing closer to her heart, the same way an infection moved through the veins.

She was so immersed in her thoughts she hadn't been paying attention to the sounds of the shower. Or lack of them. The door snapped open, and Magnus stepped out—and halted.

She wasn't sure if it was the sight of her naked body or the scars that put the stunned look on his face. She held the shirt to her chest. Her mouth opened but nothing came out but a strange squeak. He looked gorgeous, his waist wrapped in a flimsy towel with a slit up the side that showed his muscular thigh. He was holding the towel together with his fingers.

"You alright?" he asked, coming closer.

She turned away, unsure how to accept the concern she heard in his voice. Nobody had cared about her in a long time. But he had. She'd woke to find his body wrapped around hers.

Her gaze found his in the reflection. "I was checking the scars."

He came up behind her, running his fingers so lightly over the red scars she felt the barest tickle. "These are new?" he asked. When she nodded, he said, "The effects are getting worse, aren't they?" His fear over that echoed in his voice, his eyes. "You can't use it again."

"What choice do I have, if one of them is about to annihilate me? Or you?"

His fingers remained on her skin. "I can take care of myself. Just now, I thought you were dying. It was an awful feeling, not being able to do anything but wait."

Yes, he cared about her. She could see it, hear it, and feel it right to the core of her soul. He hardly knew her, and what he did know couldn't be appealing.

"I'm all right." *This time.*

He slowly traced his fingers down the center of her back, gauging her reaction. She shivered as she realized she was naked. He stopped short of going down to her behind, trailing up the indent of her spine and rubbing the back of her neck. He still held his towel together with his other hand.

"You said my name when you were seducing Lanna," she said, her voice thick.

"Because *you* were touching me."

"Not me. Lanna." But she had given away that it was mostly her by signaling him.

His mouth curved into a slight smile. "No, you. I saw *you* in there, and that's what I focused on. Too much, apparently. I almost blew it."

He gently worked the tight muscles at her neck, and she had to keep from leaning back against him. "Why didn't you say Jessie's name? She's the one in your cells."

"She's not in my cells so much anymore."

Erica wanted to keep Jessie between them, like when they'd had sex and his uttering her name kept her from feeling more than she should have. "Tell me about her. Two men were fighting over her?"

He kept up the languid movements, never taking his gaze from hers in the reflection. "I stretched the truth because I didn't want them knowing about Jessie. She's part Callorian too. Her uncle was hunting her down. He became a black beast, and I tried to fight him. He killed me."

Her eyes widened at that. "Then how…"

"She healed me. But she Holds Darkness, inherited it from her father. To heal me, she had to send it into me. I think that's why she was in my cells. It's the only explanation for my preoccupation with her."

"So, have you always been a good liar?"

"When I have to be. I won't lie to you. Ask me anything." A challenge.

"What you told Lanna about not being able to love a woman, that you'd never been in love."

He trailed his hand down her back again, spreading his fingers to cover more area. "That was true. I've been infatuated, I guess you'd call it, but never in love. I was twenty before I was able to go out in the world. I had this idea that I needed to make up for lost time, if you know what I mean. After a while, I started wanting more. But now I can't love a woman because of Darkness. I felt possessive over Jessie, and she was never mine. Hell, we never even kissed."

Erica liked the idea of that. "So what do you want now?"

His hand paused at the base of her back, and his eyes grew heavy. "I *don't* want to see the pain and loneliness of a woman's soul and feel the need to take it away, to erase every bad thing that ever happened to her." He moved closer, dipping his mouth to her shoulder and planting an exquisitely soft kiss there. "To touch her in a way she's never been touched before, make her take pleasure in a way she's never allowed herself."

She turned, dropping the shirt and slipping her arms up around his shoulders. His arms went around her waist at the same time that his mouth came down to claim hers. His towel dropped, and she felt how much he did want everything he'd just spoken about. How much he wanted *her*. She stepped out of her box a little more this time, running her tongue against his, wanting to devour him.

As vile as Lanna had been, Erica tried to remember what she'd said about a man wanting her so badly he would push a woman against a wall and thrust his pulsing rod of manhood into her right then and there. Had Magnus ever done that?

He slid his hands lower, squeezing her behind and pulling her flush against him. "I do want you that badly," he murmured. "And no, I've never wanted a woman like that before." He opened his eyes, meeting her confused gaze. "You didn't wonder that aloud, did you?"

She drew out the word, "No."

He tightened his hold on her. "I pick up thoughts."

"Like a mind reader?"

"I guess, but only random bits. I knew what you were thinking about with only a few words." His mouth, with its cupid's bow, curved into a sexy smile, and he hoisted her up onto the dresser, his hands guiding her thighs to brace his hips. "I could take you right here, slam you against the mirror and make the walls shake."

The thought of that kind of frenzied lovemaking trickled through her. "But…"

He braced her behind and moved to the bed. "This isn't going to be like those other times, Erica. Lights are on. I'm touching you. You're touching me. And you won't be sending me away afterward, got it?"

She couldn't help the smile from forming, which oddly made him smile even though he'd been oh-so-very-stern with his conditions. "Yes, sir."

He laid her down on the bed, coming with her. His damp curls felt cool as they brushed her cheeks when he leaned low and kissed her again. "You have a beautiful smile. I want to see it a lot over the next hour, which is all we've got."

She was caught in a dream and a nightmare all at once. Right now she wanted to focus on the dream. "Let's see what you can do."

It seemed odd stretching out next to him and touching him, but in an exhilarating way. She slung her leg over his and ran her hands from his mouth all the way down to his amazing chest and the ridges of his abs to his…pulsing rod of manhood.

He laughed, taking in the smile she couldn't contain. "Do they really call the cock that in those books?"

She smacked his shoulder. "Stop reading my thoughts!"

"I can't help it. That phrase just popped into my mind."

She didn't have the heart to be annoyed at him, especially not now. "I don't know if they use that phrase. I've never been interested in reading one. But now I have a living, breathing perfect male specimen, so I don't need to. Except I'm not well versed in anything but the actual act."

"We can work on that. What you're doing feels just right."

It amazed her that touching him could feel so good for her, too. His fingers traced circles up and down her sides, and then over her breasts. She stiffened slightly, and he paused, stilling his hand on her.

"I'm not used to someone touching me there," she said.

"No, I recall that. Do you trust me, Erica?"

"With every cell in my body."

That really made him smile. He pushed her back and straddled her waist, keeping his weight from crushing her. His fingers twined with hers, pressing them against the bed. He buried his face in her neck, nibbling, trailing his tongue down her neck. Slowly he made his way to her breasts, teasing at the edges, his mouth hot on her cool skin.

She squeezed his hands as the usual discomfort came and then went. Her body relaxed, and she gave into the pleasure he was giving her. Sensing that—or probably reading her thoughts, damn him—he moved on to circle her nipples with his tongue, building a whole different kind of discomfort. A delicious kind.

He released her hands and skimmed his down her sides to her hips. He moved across her stomach, dipping his tongue into her belly button, and then nibbled at the sensitive skin of her inner thighs as he nudged them apart. Oh, yeah, he was pushing her right out of her box. And he knew it. She'd always been cognizant of the irony that having sex with a stranger wasn't intimate, but letting said stranger touch her breasts or put his mouth on her was beyond her limits.

Magnus, however, was no longer a stranger.

He gripped her hips and between those innocent kisses asked, "Still trust me?"

She pushed out the word, "Yes."

His mouth came down on her, sending waves of pleasure even before he flicked her nub with his tongue. He worked magic with that tongue, making her fingers curl into the sheets and her breath come in shallow pants.

"Still trusting…you…" she uttered. "Oh, yes, *really* trusting you."

He chuckled, making his breath puff against a nub so sensitive it almost sent her over the edge. Then he did this little thing with his tongue that did. As her body shuddered with pleasure, he continued making his magic and sent her off again. He kissed his way back up her body, leaning to the side to grab a condom from his nightstand.

"Can I put it on you?" she asked, pushing him back to the bed. This time she was the one straddling, squeezing his hips with her thighs as she started to open the package. She totally got Lanna's lust, her need for sensual pleasure, because she felt it, too. Looking at Magnus did that, lying beneath her, his mouth still pink from pleasuring her, his curls on the pillow. "How can you look like an innocent boy and like sin at the same time?"

"I work very hard at it," he said with a grin. "I'm glad to see it's effective."

She leaned down to put the condom on but put her mouth on him instead. She knew the concept but not the nuances. Still, she seemed to be doing just fine by the sighs and soft groans coming from him.

Before he might go off, she pulled away and rolled the condom down over the length of him. She remembered how he'd felt inside her, the biggest man she'd ever been with. The way he had filled her had been more than his size. She had felt *something* with him, that elusive 'something' she sought with every man.

Satisfaction on a deeper level than the physical. The Stones song Magnus had played for her rolled through her mind, only she heard, *I can get satisfaction.*

She eased onto him, feeling not only that something, but being filled by a man she had feelings for. And who had feelings for her, too.

As she moved with him, his hands on her hips, she said, "Florence and the Machine is my favorite band. They have a song called *Say My Name*. I want to hear you say *my* name."

He reached up, brushing a strand of hair from her cheek. "Erica. Beautiful, brave Erica, who's making me feel things I have no business feeling."

She was afraid of him feeling possessive about her, yet it thrilled her, too. They moved together, and he whispered her name over and over, just for her. He pulled her down and turned them so that he was on top of her, body to body and face to face, as they continued to move in a sensuous rhythm.

"Is it true that you can go for hours and hours?" she asked in a teasing voice.

"Mm, aye, it is. But we don't have hours, I'm afraid."

Suddenly she wished they did, hours and days to tangle in the sheets.

"Me, too," he said, kissing her neck.

She slapped his behind. "That is maddening."

"Sorry, I'm not mindful of it. But look at the bright side: I can always give you exactly what you need."

Always. A word that sounded permanent. They didn't have permanent. They weren't even sure they had more hours to figure out what to do with those explosives.

Right then, she couldn't think about that. Only Magnus, surrounding her it seemed with his powerful body. Thrusting faster and faster, his mouth on hers and that crazy sensation building in her core, rattling her bones, and then pleasure rocketing through her.

And him, whispering her name as he came, gripping her so hard he might never let her go. The crazier thought? She didn't want him to.

# CHAPTER 16

Magnus pulled her tight against him as they both caught their breath. Her head rested on his chest, her hand on his stomach. She felt good there. So good he didn't want to let her go.

He twined his fingers with hers. "After I'd been infected with Darkness, I slept with a lot of woman to try to drive Jessie out of my cells."

Erica sat up, her expression one of mock consternation. "Magnus, you're a charmer, no doubt about it, but you've got to work on your during and post-coital bedside manner."

He knew she was kidding, sort of, but he couldn't find a smile. "You did it. I no longer feel her or anything but happiness for her and my brother. The problem is, I can feel you"—he rubbed his chest—"here, in that same way. I want to protect you, to keep you safe, but I'm feeling that possessiveness, too. Like I don't want you to leave this bed. Like I want to *consume* you so I can keep you inside me."

It grew big and dark inside him, clawing at him from the inside and growing stronger with every second he held her. He sat up, planting his feet on the floor and rubbing his fingers through his curls. "Remember what

I told you, God, that was only last night. You're better off despising me."

She sat up too, putting her hand against his broad back. "I tangle with killers. You think I'm going to run from *you*?"

He turned to her. "I'm a killer, too. And I could end up hurting you." A knock sounded at the door. "It's Pope and Suza." Thank God he'd knocked and not popped right in. "Give us a minute." Magnus jabbed his finger at her. "No more going after murderers. You're done with that business, do you understand? I know I don't own you, but I do care about you." He got up and grabbed his pants before heading into the bathroom to clean up. "I won't have you killing yourself."

She quickly pulled on his T-shirt and her pants. "Is this part of your Darkness or are you always this bossy?"

"It's probably both."

She took him in as he came back into the room. "I think it's just you. It goes with your protectiveness."

"Either way, I'm now dangerous to you."

"I can handle what you are. As you reasoned to Lanna, I'm the only woman who understands you. Who's not afraid of what you are."

His expression shadowed. "*I'm* afraid of what I am." He opened the door to allow Pope and his friend in.

Twenty minutes later, they'd all gotten up to speed as they sat in various places in his tiny room. Magnus laid a map out on the bed, and Pope marked where the main group of Callorians were living.

Magnus drew a line with a pen. "The tunnel goes southeast in this area through Strasford."

Pope took the pen and marked a perpendicular line across that one. “This is where we sensed the boundary of Darkness falling away. Let’s assume it covers this area.” He drew a large circle.

“The entire town,” Suza said on a low breath.

Pope glanced at his watch. “Torus was calling a meeting right about now. We need to know what’s going on, but I don’t know if I can ‘port there.”

“I’ll astral project and spy on the meeting,” Magnus said.

Pope, who now looked like a guy who should be in a rock band, nodded. “Carry on with it.”

Well, except for his talking like that.

Magnus reclined on the bed. “It’s been a while since I’ve done it.” After his brother got trapped at the Battle of Culloden, Magnus hadn’t been so keen on sending his soul straying. He felt someone sit beside him and cracked his eye open. Erica, with a worried expression, had settled in so close her thigh touched his arm. She cared about him, too. It warmed him—and scared him.

He put his hand on her leg, gave it a squeeze, and settled into his mind. He imagined the place on the map and the buildings Pope had described. His soul lightened, then pulled away from the heaviness of the Darkness and the density of his body. For the first time in a week, he didn’t feel that wretched black feeling.

He focused on the surroundings that slowly came into focus. The place he popped into resembled what Pope had described, a remote area that looked like an industrial park. The last of the day’s rays washed pink over the sand and sparse vegetation. People were trailing into the building in front of him. Magnus ducked back against the side of that building. To those at his target location, he appeared ghost-like. He didn't want them to be alerted to his presence. Most of the faces he saw showed no emotion, but he spotted some who appeared to be concerned. When the last straggler had gone inside, he projected inside.

The large room was set up with rows of chairs facing a podium. Magnus stood in the small kitchen where people fixed a cup of coffee in Styrofoam cups and snagged cookies. Heh. They weren't so different from the humans here after all. He tucked himself in the corner and tried to tune into the soft chatter of people speculating as to what was going on.

Before long, a man stepped to the podium. He didn't make a sound, but suddenly everyone went to their chairs and settled in. So that must be Torus, the man in charge.

Torus looked at a man near the door. "Is everyone accounted for?"

"No, sir." He consulted his clipboard. "Swanson has not checked in. Nor have any of the Strasford contingent."

Lanna, Copeland, and Nester. Swanson was probably the guy Pope killed in the tunnel. So they didn't know about the bodies yet.

"Try rousing them on their phones. It's important that everyone be here." Torus turned to the audience. "We have been here for many years on a very important mission. It has not always been easy. A few of our people have gone missing and still haven't been located. You have given up your homes to live here in the desert, and for that your government is thankful. You will be rewarded well."

A smattering of applause broke out, and Torus continued. “Of course, your discretion will continue to be necessary. You are among the very few who are privy to what we are doing here. You can imagine how our citizens would react if they knew we’ve been tapping into their own repressed emotions for the energy we sell to them. As the mass of Darkness has trickled through the finestra these past years, it has caused a serious resource problem in Surfacia. I am happy to report that we are very, very close to pushing the mass back through the finestra to our dimension.”

More applause broke out, and Torus allowed it to go on for several seconds. Magnus sorted through what he’d heard. Darkness creeping into this dimension and infecting the people of Strasford, just as Pope suspected.

Torus and the man at the door exchanged some nonverbal communication. The men hadn’t been found. Torus indicated that he should conduct a search and then faced the audience. “As you know, we planned for a seven-day evacuation, detonating the explosives right before we exit through the finestra north of here. Darkness, however, is spreading faster than we anticipated and jeopardizing our plan. It’s beginning to collapse the tunnels south of our Strasford monitoring station.

“If the explosives detonate from the southern point, it will send the mass of Darkness toward us and our escape finestra rather than the one we’ve planned. So we are moving up our departure time. You have three hours to pack your belongings and meet at the finestra.”

Panic rippled through the audience, nearly knocking Magnus right out of the projection.

"You will all go safely through before we start the explosions," Torus continued. "Anyone left behind will suffer the same devastation as this entire area. This is one example of why it's imperative to follow the rules I have set out. You are dismissed."

Magnus pulled out, waking up with three people staring at him. He sat up and rubbed his face, getting used to the density of his body again—and Darkness. "You want the bad news first or the really bad news?" He didn't wait for their response. "We have to disable those explosives before they take out the entire area. And we have three hours to do it." He filled them in on everything he'd heard.

Pope leaned over the map and marked two F's near each end of the tunnel line they'd drawn. "So their plan is to push Darkness back through this finestra while they escape through this one."

Suza followed the line with her painted nail. "Which is going to take out the town of Strasford. My friend. Everyone."

Magnus hated to say it, but they needed to know. "And more bad news: they're looking for the missing people, so they'll probably find the body of the guy you killed, Pope. They'll be on alert, which is going to make it even harder for us to infiltrate it." He took them in. "So we have a choice. We have enough time to escape and save our asses. We could try to warn people to leave the area because of an impending earthquake, but without credentials the effectiveness of that is unlikely."

"Or," Erica said, "we try our damned best to at least put a gap between the explosives so that maybe it won't be a chain reaction. Limit the damage."

Pope leaned closer to the map. “But we need to send Darkness back to the other dimension. It’s causing a lot of problems here and will continue to. If I can start the detonation with my Flare here, north of Strasford, we can send it through the finestra that Torus is planning to evacuate through. If we leave enough of a gap between Strasford and everything south of there, the town will be spared.”

Suza said, “It may cause damage, like a small earthquake would, but at least it won’t be mass destruction. So we go down into the tunnel, gather the explosives between here and there.” She pointed to the tunnel line. “Start the explosion and do that freaky ‘port thing to get us out of here.”

Pope’s expression turned grim. “If it works.”

Magnus said, “And if it doesn’t, we die. That’s a given. Are you all ready to make that kind of sacrifice?”

Erica’s mouth tightened in determination. “If we don’t, a lot of people are going to die. What if the explosion affects Vegas?”

Magnus knew Erica would be onboard. She’d been sacrificing herself to save others for years. He hated the idea of it, though. He knew Pope would be in, too.

Suza said, “I couldn’t live with myself if I just hightailed it out to save my own fanny.” She gave Pope a private smile. “I’m so in.”

Magnus said, “I bet the finestra is close to the house where we were held captive. When we went down into the tunnel, I felt a weird sensation.”

Pope tapped one of the *F’s*. “Do not get too close to it. Finestras pull in what belongs there. Darkness.

Callorians. Since you have our DNA it might pull you in, but your body wouldn't survive the travel."

"If the finestra naturally pulls in what belongs, why is Torus using the explosives to send Darkness back?" Magnus asked.

"Because it is such a huge mass, it will need help. The explosives are meant to guide it in the right direction. Torus has laid in much more material than he needs to ensure it happens. The destruction of cities and people doesn't matter to him; only his mission does. Suza and I will reduce the number of those devices leading from Strasford toward Vegas while you and Erica start from the other end. We will meet in the middle, as we did earlier. We'll need a receptacle to collect the explosives so we can take them with us."

"It's a plan," Magnus said. "A crazy-assed, risky, and probably doomed plan, but the only one we have. Remember that we may encounter our enemy." He turned to Erica. "You cannot use your Lightning. *I need you.*" His heart hitched. "To stay alive, okay?"

She nodded. "I'll find some other weapon."

Magnus tore his gaze from her and turned to the map. "We'll start at the house. I want to make sure Lanna got released. I'm sure she'll be mad as hell at us, but she's obviously not devoted to this group. I suspect she'll save her own ass rather than take us down."

Pope said, "I'll 'port you there first and then take Suza farther up the tunnel."

"No, save your power. We're going to need it at the end when it counts. The house isn't far from here. I'll project and figure out where it is."

Suza handed him a set of keys. "This one is for my truck. Please be careful. It's almost paid off." She released the dream catcher key ring. "I know, that truck's safety is the least of my worries, right?"

Magnus chuckled. "I'll be careful."

Pope clasped his hand over Suza's. "Let's synchronize our watches." They did, and in a blink the two were gone.

Erica stared at where they'd just been. "If it weren't for all the other craziness I've seen, that would totally blow my mind."

Magnus settled back on the bed and imagined that basement cage. What he saw propelled him right back into his body and upright. "Shite. Bloody hell. Son of a *bitch*." His stomach felt like a gaping hole inside him. He turned to Erica, who was clearly waiting for him to tell her what he'd seen. "Nester killed her. She was still locked in the cell…what was left of her. He's gone mad, tore her apart."

"Oh, God." She put her hand to her mouth. "You didn't know what would happen. How could you?"

"Still, I left her there." He thrashed himself with guilt, even as he knew Erica was right. "Nester wasn't at the meeting, so he doesn't know about the new deadline. Hopefully he's at the house. I need to go back and pinpoint the location."

He dreaded seeing the scene again, but they would soon be there in person. The moment he projected into the basement, he floated up through the living room and roof, then far above it. Not surprisingly, the house was by itself at the edge of civilization. Magnus was able to see several signs, and he followed those streets to the main one. He extracted himself, feeling the familiar fatigue tugging at him. "Let's go."

They pulled up to the house twenty minutes later. A sedan sat out front.

Magnus turned to Erica. "We have to be ready for Nester. And you—"

"Can't use my Lightning, I know."

He hoped she did know. "You have no weapon you can use against him when he's in Darkness. You have to leave it to me." He could see her resistance to that. "I can handle myself, but if you throw yourself into the fray, it'll make me crazy."

She pushed her hair back. "All right. What if he's about to kill you? Because if you're…out of the picture, he'll go after me. I'm not going to let you die, especially when it means a death sentence for me either way. I'm going to use my Lightning."

The thought of it nearly paralyzed him. Magnus wasn't arrogant enough to know he could defeat a man who had a lot more experience using Darkness. "We have two and a half hours. Let's go."

They approached the house cautiously, Magnus watching for any movement in the windows. She carried the box of heavy duty yard-waste bags they'd picked up at the store. The front door was unlocked, and he pushed it open and went in first. Paper money littered the floor. Nester had gone mad, all right. Then Magnus heard a sound out in the garage. The hairs on the back of his neck rose, and he instinctively moved in front of Erica.

"You won't make me go back there," Nester's voice said from the garage. "Never going back!"

A black form raced out from the laundry room. Magnus Became on instinct, throwing himself out of the way—and into Erica—as Nester was about to slam into him.

"Go downstairs," Magnus whispered, though it sounded garbled in his form.

He didn't want her there, as a target.

She ran toward a door that looked like it might go down to the basement. Magnus headed Nester off as he made a go for her. Their bodies collided, sending them crashing into the couch. Nester's fangs flashed in front of Magnus's face. He backed up in the nick of time, feeling only the brush of their cool length against his shoulder.

Magnus used his enormous paw to slam Nester in the side of his head. Nester fell to the side but kicked out, slicing Magnus's arm. He felt the pain, but also the way his form began to mend itself. He glanced up and saw Erica watching from her place behind the door, terror in her eyes.

He didn't have time to wonder if it was terror at seeing his beast or the prospect of him getting hurt. Nester came at him again. Magnus threw himself on his back and used his legs to toss Nester against the glass étagère. Shards of broken glass and metal poked through his form as it collapsed, and he screeched in pain. Magnus ran to him, feeling some of those shards beneath his paws. Nester broke free just as Magnus lunged at his throat.

Nester wrapped his powerful arms around Magnus, holding him back. Magnus pictured that bloody scene below, Nester attacking a defenseless woman. It injected him with a rage that suffused him, and he managed to tear out a chunk of Nester's throat.

Nester clamped his paw over the wound. "You can't defeat me. You are less powerful than I am," he growled. "I will kill you and then I will tear your female friend apart, bite by bite after I fu—"

Magnus's rage exploded, and he cut off Nester's words with a head butt that knocked him back. "You might be more powerful," Magnus said as he went for his throat again. "But when you threaten someone I care about, you ignite my emotions. And they are far more powerful than your madness." He kept tearing at him, as Nester tried to fight him off.

Bits of Darkness scattered everywhere, like blood and matter, until there was nothing left for Nester to mend. Darkness melted away, and Magnus dropped to the floor to catch his breath.

Erica ran to his side, staring at what was left of Nester, who had returned to his mangled human form, and then at him.

"Yes, this is what I am." He searched for the fear and disdain he had seen in her eyes before. "A beast, as you said."

She knelt down beside him, brushing the skin next to the gash that hadn't had time to completely mend. "A beast who saved my life." She kissed his cheek. "We'd better go."

His heart opened as he came to his feet, even as he had to shut it again. He would not subject her to what he was, no matter the gift she had just given him.

Erica stopped dead midway down the stairs, frozen by the sight of the carnage. He stepped in front of her, blocking the view. She put her hand on his shoulder. "It's not your fault. Nester did this. You did what you had to do to save us."

He would have killed Lanna with his own hands to save them. Painful, but the truth. They went down into the tunnel.

Torus checked his watch. Everything was in place, even with the timeframe moved up. Still, he felt anxious, which wasn't like him. He rarely felt anything. But he had worked so long and hard out in this godforsaken desert, dealing with behavioral issues, missing men, and being away from home, all for this. He needed to return triumphant.

Some officer at the other end of the finestra was working just as diligently on the containment system for Darkness. Torus wondered if he were worried, too. Swanson's disappearance was more concerning. He wasn't one of the troublemakers, unlike Copeland, who had piqued his suspicion recently. His not reporting that Darkness was infecting the residents of the town in ways that would draw media attention bothered him most. His brother was even more troublesome, always on edge. The fact that the entire household hadn't shown for the meeting didn't bode well.

He teletransported to their house. He didn't recognize the bright red truck in the driveway. Everyone in his group owned subdued vehicles that didn't attract attention. On alert, he entered the premises and found a room full of shattered furniture and broken glass. But nothing as shattered as the body in the corner. The thrum of concern grew stronger within his chest. He thought it was Nester.

He searched the house, finding packed suitcases and a stash of twenty, fifty, and hundred dollar bills.

Money they would not need back in Surfacia. He went downstairs into the basement and encountered a scene even more gruesome. He remembered Lanna's white-blond hair, and the few tufts that were not stained with blood were that color.

With the tunnel door open, Swanson's disappearance now held even more ominous overtones. Torus called his new second-in-command—his first had also gone missing last month. "We have trouble. Sound the alarm and tell everyone to meet at the finestra immediately. But don't sound it in the tunnel. We're moving up detonation."

"We still have two people in the tunnel: Swanson and Yurek, who went to look for him."

"If they're not back in time, we'll have to proceed anyway." Torus closed the door to the tunnel and pushed the latch in, then 'ported back to the detonation switch at headquarters.

# CHAPTER 17

Pope and Suza worked their way down the tunnel, pulling down those sinister white boxes and stuffing them into the trash bag they each carried. Hers was getting so heavy that she had to drag it.

Pope moved faster than she did but kept glancing back to keep an eye on her. Every so often they would trade places so they remained close. He might be from another dimension. He might be scary and a killer, but he was risking his life to save others. People he didn't even know.

"You are thinking good thoughts about me," he said, pulling down another box. "I like the way it feels."

"Yeah, me, too. I just hope we get to explore this thing between us."

"I want to take you on a date." He said the word 'date' as though he'd never used it before. "I have heard a lot about dates. I think I will find them enjoyable."

He gave her such a goofy, innocent smile she had to laugh. Which doused the smile.

"I have a lot to learn," he said. "Petra took me to task for calling a date a social interaction with sexual motivation."

"Mm, I can understand how that might dampen the fire. Except for the sexual part. I hope we can explore that, too."

Pope made a cute sound in his throat but continued with his task.

A noise echoed down the tunnel in the direction of the compound. Pope came up beside her, all protective, and watched the dim lights. A black panther materialized, coming up fast. Pope stepped in front of her.

The panther came to a stop only a few feet away and materialized to the man they'd seen earlier in Strasford. The one who would kill Pope.

Yurek gave him a phony smile. "Fancy meeting you here. I thought you might have something to do with Swanson's disappearance." He took in the bags filled with the white boxes. "Torus would have your head, but I have no intention of letting him know about you. You think you can stop this? There are miles of explosives."

He turned into one of the ugliest wolves she had ever seen and lunged at Pope. The two fell to the ground, the wolf's mouth clamped around Pope's wrist. Blood dripped down his arm as they tussled. Pope thrust out his hand. A glow emanated from his palm and then fizzled out.

He couldn't blast the guy. Suza's heart tightened into a tiny ball as she watched the two fight, unarmed man and a wolf-creature with sharp teeth that kept swiping toward Pope's throat.

She took out her gun, tucked in her waistband, and inched closer. She had to shoot where the bullet would go straight into the wall and not down the tunnel. Following their movements, inching closer, she aimed.

Pope threw Yurek, bumping into her and knocking her to her ass. The gun fell to the ground a few feet away. Yurek's snout-full of teeth came at her, but Pope dragged him back. He wouldn't 'port away. Not only because he wanted to save his power, but she knew in her heart that he wouldn't leave her there. She scrambled on hands and knees to where the gun landed in the shadows.

She turned, crouching, and readied. *Please don't let me hit Pope by mistake.*

Pope got the upper hand with the beast, wrestling it to the ground. It wasn't defeated though. It pulled back its hind legs, claws sharp and extended, and readied to push Pope off.

"Suza, wait," he gritted out and slapped his palm to the beast's head. A small Flare threw it back. It hit the wall and became Yurek again. He started to shift back.

"Now," Pope said.

She pulled the trigger. The blast echoed, jabbing into her head like a boxing glove. Pope jumped to his feet, surveying the dead man.

"Nicely done," he said.

She tapped the handle. "Good to know the human weapon can kick otherworldly ass."

"Pope!" Magnus's voice, a distance down the tunnel.

"We're all right," Suza shouted. Profound relief washed over her. They were almost ready. And they still had an hour to spare.

Two silhouettes, dragging their full bags like Santa Clauses, materialized in the gloom.

Magnus said, "I figure we're on the north end of Strasford. I can still feel Darkness."

Pope took them all in with their bags. "Put your hands on my arm. I should be able to bring us close to the compound."

In a flash, they were back where they'd started taking down the explosive devices. Pope looked relieved. He still had one more very important 'port to do. Or else they died, but she didn't want to think about that.

Pope rubbed his hands together. "This is going to take split-second timing. You all must be ready, hands on me and on your bags. The moment I set this device off, we're out of here. If the bags are left behind, there will still be enough explosives to damage the town."

She hated this part of the plan, not that any part of it was great. Pope would start the blast with his Flare on the first device, sending the chain reaction toward the compound. They'd taken enough of the explosives out along the way so that it wouldn't extend outward much.

A man materialized in front of them. His eyes widened as he took in four strangers. "Who are you people, and why are you sabotaging my project?"

"Because the people here shouldn't die for our mistakes, Torus," Pope said.

He narrowed his eyes. "You're one of us, but they are not." He saw the bags with the square devices pushing against the plastic. "I will not allow you to destroy everything I've worked years to put into place." He held out his hand, and there was nothing wrong with *his* glow. "In ten minutes everything will be detonated, so you've failed anyway."

Suza shot him, throwing him back several feet. "I know I took a chance," she said, rushing the words together. "But I couldn't let him kill us. Not after all the work *we've* done."

Magnus stepped up next to Pope. "You didn't even try to zap him."

"My Flare isn't as strong as I'd like." He flexed his hand and tried to summon it. Hardly a glimmer. "I've overused my powers. I won't be able to detonate the devices."

Suza lifted her gun. "I'll shoot one."

They got into position, and she aimed at the first device on the wall. *Click.* She checked the gun. "Hell. Empty."

"I'll do it."

Everyone turned to Erica. She was holding out her hand, a glow pulsing in her palm. "I have enough power."

Magnus said, "No, you—"

"I know I'll die. So go now, all of you. Take everything. As soon as you're gone I'll set them off. That way you're safe." She gripped Magnus's arm. "It's the only way. You heard him. They're going to set it off in ten minutes. *Go.*"

Magnus's voice was raw when he said, "I'm not going without you."

Erica gave Pope a secret nod that told him to make sure Magnus went. "Magnus, I was going to end up dying anyway. So now I can save a lot more lives than one killer would have taken."

A sound caught their attention. Torus had crawled to the bag closest to him and was reaching for one of the devices. His hand glowed. He was going to set it off—

Suza felt that now-familiar *whoosh* and blinked, finding herself on the hill where they'd scoped out the compound. The sound of an explosion riveted her attention below. The ground erupted, as though a gigantic earthworm was making its way toward them. Each device exploded in domino fashion, just as planned. But those explosions were coming toward the compound. Wherever there was an explosion, the ground collapsed in a several-yards wide swath, shaking the sand in either direction for a mile.

What hovered above the ground was even wilder. A dark mist shimmered like heat, a wave of it rolling toward the compound.

"Darkness," Pope said.

She looked at their group, Magnus and Erica and all their bags. Magnus had his arms around Erica, holding her fast against his chest. Suza stepped closer to Pope, needing that connection as she turned back to the devastation below.

It reached the compound, buildings and cars falling into the gaping hole. She saw no people; they'd all been evacuated. The explosions finally stopped, but the wave of Darkness kept going, drawn toward that portal thing Pope talked about.

High like a tidal wave, it washed over the mountain next to theirs and disappeared right into it. The mountains shuddered. Magnus took a halted breath and stumbled back, as though someone had punched him. Erica turned in his arms, and he shook his head. "I'm fine. The air got thin all of a sudden. I couldn't breathe."

Pope surveyed the area. “I don’t feel Darkness. It’s gone.” He gestured to the bags. “I have to take these back to my dimension. They’re too dangerous to leave here.”

Suza now sucked in a breath. “But from everything you’ve told me it’s too dangerous for you to go back there.”

Pope touched her chin. “I have to. I cannot risk anyone finding these explosives. They are made from materials not of this dimension. I will take you to your truck, and then I’ll go to the finestra on the south side of Strasford.”

“We’ll go,” Magnus said. “And we’ll wait for you to come back.”

Forty minutes later, Magnus watched Pope step into what looked like a wall of shimmering heat and disappeared.

Suza leaned against the front of the truck, wringing her fingers. “Will he come back?”

“If he can, he will.” Magnus squeezed her shoulder. “He has a reason.” Unless he was caught, but no need to mention that.

They’d stopped at a store where they bought coats and a pair of shoes for Suza. The night air bit into his cheeks and stung his lips. He took Erica’s hand. “We’ll be right back.”

He pulled her away, though not out of sight of Suza. He then tugged her into his arms. “That was the maddest, bravest thing I’ve ever seen. *You* are the maddest, bravest thing I’ve seen.”

"I was scared to death to die. I've spent a lot of years taking that sort of risk, willing to die for a good cause. But I've never had anything to live for." She tilted her head, the breeze blowing her hair across her cheek. "And I don't care if you've got Darkness, that you turn into a beast or that you'll get wildly possessive. I can deal with that."

He started to protest her willingness to once again put herself in harm's way, but no words came out. Because he realized something. He stepped back and patted his stomach. "I don't feel it."

"Feel what?"

"Darkness. I don't feel the heaviness." He held out his hand and stared at it, summoning the lion. Nothing. "I don't have it anymore. I don't have it!" He swung her into his arms and spun her around. "It must have gone when the whole of it went. Remember when I sucked in that breath? I felt something pass through me. But I was so preoccupied with everything else, I didn't realize the dark heaviness wasn't in me anymore."

She leaned down and kissed him, a beautiful light in her eyes.

"You would have stayed with me anyway," he said, feeling that sacrifice as much as the one she'd almost made in the tunnel. "Even though I was a beast."

She put her hand to his cheek. "*You* weren't a beast."

She hadn't always felt that way, but he wasn't about to remind her. "Come home with me to Maryland. I need to see my brother."

She gave him a teasing smile. "And Jessie?"

"Who?"

She kissed him again. “I’d love to come home with you.”

Suza was watching them, a wistful smile on her face. They joined her, and he could pick up her worried thoughts about Pope. She really cared about him. He knew Pope cared about her, too.

An hour passed, the longest of their lives. “He’s not coming back,” Suza said, her arms tight around her waist. “The best man I ever fell in love with, and he’s gone.” Tears glittered on her eyelashes and spilled down cheeks red from the cold.

Magnus pulled her close. “Don’t give up yet.”

“I haven’t given up, I just…oh, Magnus, it’s not looking good.”

Her grief vibrated through him. He reached out and grasped Erica’s hand, pulling her up next to him. She patted Suza’s back, clearly as uncomfortable with this comforting business as he was.

Erica sucked in a breath, pointing. The air shimmered in the weird way it had when Pope had gone through. He stepped out of the finestra, looking the way he had when they’d first met: shaved head, tall, and with violet eyes. Suza rushed toward him, which baffled Magnus because as far as he knew, she’d only seen him the way he’d looked when he left.

“You’re back,” she said, running her fingers over her face. “I like you this way.”

“My façade stripped away when I entered my dimension. I took on my old one when I came back.” He held Suza tight for a few moments, squeezing his eyes shut. Finally he moved back. “The group who was here never made it back. Darkness exploded as it went through the finestra, most likely taking everyone with it. The government will have to come clean, I suppose, and explain why they no longer have the power they once did. But that is not my problem." He gave them a guileless smile. "I have a date to prepare for."

"A lot of them," Suza said, her gaze never leaving him.

"I'm going back to Maryland," Magnus said, pressing Erica's hand to his mouth. "*We're* going back. Amy will be having her baby any moment now. And I need to see Lachlan."

Pope laced his fingers with Suza's. "Suza, you'll come with me to Maryland? I'd like you to meet my family."

Her cheeks flushed, and she nodded. "But I have to bail Carlene out of jail."

"I have ways of clearing up those kinds of matters." He turned back to Magnus and Erica. "We'll visit, but I believe I'll be returning here for a few weeks."

Suza leaned closer to Pope. "Months. Years."

He smiled. "Yes, years sounds good." He glanced up into the night sky. "I like it here." Then he looked at Suza. "Very much."

Magnus chuckled, finding it odd to see Pope…well, in love. "Good for you. Both of you." He turned to Erica. "Good for us, too. I'm thinking months. Years. Who knows? My life is full of possibilities again. And I happen to like the possibility right in front of me."

She kissed him, something he treasured because he knew how hard doing that had once been for her.

They all crammed into Suza's truck and drove to Magnus's BMW, which was still parked at the trailhead. Where Erica had followed him because she thought he was a killer. It was almost laughable now. Everything had happened just the way it was supposed to, though. Aye, he believed in fate.

Erica stared down the trail, her expression dark.

He came up behind her. "Thinking of the man Nester killed?"

She nodded, but broke out of the thought. "Let's get out of here."

He opened the door and pulled out his phone. "I have several missed calls."

"Two will be from me," Pope said, ready to head off with Suza.

"Four are from Lachlan. Something's wrong." He listened as Lachlan told him that Amy was going into labor, and then where the birthing center was, and then another call: "I hope you're not so shattered or mad at me that you'd not come out, especially how daft you were about the baby."

Erica gave him a questioning look, and Magnus shook his head. "I wasn't *daft.* But aye, I was taken in by the whole miracle of it." There was something magical about Amy's belly growing, her body creating a person inside her. And the way Lucas held her, proud and protective, had sparked that kind of desire in Magnus, too. He deleted that call and listened to the next: Amy just had the baby. And Lachlan was worried about his brother.

Magnus's chest filled with his need to see him. He disconnected and turned to Pope, who was waiting. "Amy's had the baby. Can you work your magic one more time to take us there? I have an address."

Pope grinned. "I'll give it a try. We'll be shielded for a few seconds until I can ascertain whether anyone who should not see us appear out of thin air isn't there."

Erica said, "I can wait for you—"

"No, you're coming with me. I'm not letting you out of my sight."

"Bossy, aren't you?"

He smiled. "Aye, and it's not the Darkness. I think it's the being in love part. It's something I have to get used to. All I know is that I don't want you away from me. And I want you to meet my brother and friends."

She hesitated, then nodded. "I'll meet the guy who killed Jerryl?"

"Aye, I'm sure he'll be there. He's the new father's best friend."

The three put their hands on Pope's arm. In a *whoosh*, they stood in a cheery and very crowded room.

"What do I do with this thing?" Amy asked when the nurse set the baby in her arms. Her green eyes were huge as she stared at her baby girl. "I've been reading all the books but everything just flew right out of my head."

Lucas settled in beside her on the bed, pressing close to her. His gaze was on the baby, too. "We'll figure it out, babe. And look, we've got plenty of help." He gestured to the people around them.

The nurse patted Amy's leg. "You'll be fine, darlin'. Every new mom says the same thing, but being a parent is an innate ability. You'll make mistakes but you'll get it right most of the time." She pointed to the group. "Be quiet in here. You've all way exceeded the limit."

Petra squeezed in on Amy's other side, her face aglow as she touched the baby's cheek. "You are so beautiful, Francesca Emily Vanderwyck."

The moment the nurse exited, the shield fell away.

"Pope!"

Petra ran over and gave him a hug. Everyone turned to them, first surprise and then warmth on their faces. Lachlan, standing next to Jessie, also wore his hesitation. Magnus stalked toward him, keeping his expression neutral. Make the bastard sweat another second or two.

He grabbed hold of him and yanked him into a bear hug. "Locky."

Lachlan's arms went round him then. "Maggie."

Magnus didn't want to let him go, but he forced himself to step back. "It's alright. I'm alright." He raised his arms. "I don't Hold Darkness anymore."

Jessie stepped closer. "Thank God. But how?"

"It's a long story, and not one I'm going to dump out here. But it's gone, Pope is safe, and I'm glad to be home." He clasped his brother's shoulder. "With my brother and the woman he's probably going to marry."

Jessie's expression crumpled. "I'm so sorry—"

"Don't be. My brother is happy, and that means the world to me." He turned and gestured for Erica to come over. "I want you to meet the reason I'm happy. This is Erica. Erica Evrard." He let the name sink in. They had everyone's attention anyway, all waiting, no doubt, to see if Magnus would explode in Darkness at seeing Lachlan and Jessie. A few soft gasps sounded as he turned her toward the rest of the group. "Aye, Jerryl's sister." He introduced her to Lachlan and Jessie.

Erica shook hands with them and then studied the group. "Which one of you killed him?"

Eric stepped forward, his expression contrite. A rare thing in itself. "I did. We were in a war—"

She walked over and thrust out her hand. "Thank you."

Eric seemed to push past his shock and clasped her hand. "You're welcome."

Magnus came up behind her, draping his arms over her shoulders. "Turns out he was a bigger bastard than we thought. No need to elaborate, but suffice it to say you did the world a favor." He turned to her. "This is Eric, who's married to Fonda. She worked with Jerryl." No need either to mention that she'd dated him. "I'm not going to bombard you with everyone's names right now; you'll have time to get to know them. We're sort of family. We've been through a lot together. They're sort of your family, too. We all share the Callorian essence."

He couldn't tell what she thought about that, but her face warmed and her eyes watered. Did she have any family? Anyone in her life? Considering what she'd been doing these last years, he guessed not. Now she would, him and all of these people.

He turned her toward Amy. "But this is the reason we came so quickly. Amy and Lucas Vanderwyck, new parents. And baby Francesca."

"After Lucas's mom," Amy said, her face bright. "And Emily for my mom."

Magnus leaned down and planted a kiss on her cheek, then shook Lucas's hand. "Congratulations." Then he took in the beautiful babe in Amy's arms.

"She's brilliant." He took her tiny hand. "Pleased to meet you. Welcome to your mad family."

He turned to all of them, Olivia and Nicholas, Zoe and Rand, everyone. They were his family. It wasn't just him and Lachlan anymore.

Amy laughed, but it faded as she looked at him, Erica, and then Pope and Suza. "You will tell us why you all look as though you've been crawling around in the dirt, right? Why you're bruised and cut and look like hell. I mean, I know I look like hell, but I've been in labor for umpteen hours. You all don't have that excuse."

Magnus glanced over at Pope and Suza, with Petra planted between them, one arm around both. Then he pulled Erica close. "Later. Just know everything's okay. And now that we know you're safe, we're going back to Arizona to recover." He squeezed her hand. "And do lots of sleeping." His thumb traced a circle on her palm, and she gave him a clever smile. Aye, she got it.

Pope came over with Suza. "Yes, a lot of sleeping. We'll check back in a few days, once we attend to a few matters."

Petra gave him a sly grin. "Yeah, you have fun with that."

They clasped their hands on Pope again, all connected in a way no one but them would ever understand. Magnus touched his mouth to Erica's just before the *whoosh*.

***THE END***

# FROM THE AUTHOR

I hope you've enjoyed the (for now) last book in the Offspring series! New to the Offspring? Start from the beginning and experience all of the passion, danger, and suspense! See the sneak peek of A PERFECT DARKNESS, the first book in the Offspring series, below.

The Offspring series, in order:

A PERFECT DARKNESS

OUT OF THE DARKNESS

TOUCHING DARKNESS

BURNING DARKNESS

BEYOND THE DARKNESS

DARKNESS BECOMES HER

And two novellas (that dovetail into the events of THE END OF DARKNESS)

THE DARKNESS WITHIN

TURN TO DARKNESS

THE END OF DARKNESS

Go to www.JaimeRush.com for all the details on the Offspring, as well as my paranormal romantic suspense series from Grand Central Publishing—The Hidden.

Miami. A melting pot of cultures: American, Cuban, Haitian…Dragons, Angels, and sorcerers. Magick hides behind the glitter and sunshine, where humans imbued with the essence of deities keep the balance between angry and forgotten gods, demons, and those of their kind who cannot fight the seductive lure of their magick.

For romantic suspense with a touch of paranormal, check out my Tina Wainscott e-books, available in most formats.

Meet the men of The Justiss Alliance ~ Here to serve, protect, and rock your world.

When five Navy SEALs take the fall for a covert mission gone wrong, this kick-butt brotherhood joins The Justiss Alliance, a private agency that exacts justice outside the law.

Details at www.TinaWainscott.com

# A PERFECT DARKNESS

## CHAPTER 1

"Mr. Bromley, there's no need to fling yourself out of the window." Amy Shane covered her cockatoo's cage with the obnoxious bright orange blanket before he started squawking, like he did whenever she was on the phone. "I have a ninety-five percent retrieval rate." Her love life might be non-existent, and her plan to eat healthier was feeble at best, but she was damned good at saving people's data.

"My presentation is on that drive. My only copy, I know, I'm an idiot for not backing it up, and then to drop it—" He let out an agonized groan.

She returned to the second bedroom of her apartment, cracked open the laptop case, and studied the damp interior. "And how did it end up in a pool…you know what, I don't want to know. Is there anything else on the drive that you need?"

"There's one folder titled *Upcoming Issues* that's rather important. Just business documents, but of a, ah, sensitive nature."

She knew he was lying about the folder's contents.

Whatever it contained held significant emotional relevance…and the potential to embarrass him. She didn't really want to know that. She didn't want to see the green glow that told her he was hiding something.

She plugged the hard drive into her computer. "I'd better start working on it."

"You'll call—"

"The moment I know what we have," she assured.

"I hope so," he said, his voice and glow emanating anxiety; if she didn't retrieve his data, she might have to do some suicide counseling. Wouldn't be the first time.

It was bad enough seeing people's glows—what she later learned were called auras—when she was physically with them. That had started when she was a kid, seeing her teacher's yellow glow and knowing the woman was sad, and then doing the really dumb thing and trying to comfort her. Which freaked the woman out and taught Amy a more important lesson than math or reading: seeing colors that indicated people's moods or intentions, was weird.

In the last few years they'd gotten pervasive. Everywhere she went, she saw that smoky mist. Oh, how people lied and hid their pain, and how that deceit made her distrustful. That was why she worked out of her home and hardly saw anyone. Except now she was seeing glows through the frickin' phone!

She uncovered Orn'ry's cage. He made happy clicking sounds, and his "crown" of white feathers sprang to attention when she opened his door. "Okay, you can come into my office now." She held out her arm, and Orn'ry climbed aboard. She sat down at her work table, and he climbed up to her shoulder. She liked working to alternative rock cranked loud. For Orn'ry's sake she slipped on her headphones.

Orn'ry pecked at the ear piece. "Stop it," she growled. Then he pecked her nose. "Ow!" She shooed him off, and he fluttered to his stand. He wasn't called ornery for nothing. That's how he'd ended up at the animal shelter where she volunteered. No one could stand him, and he languished, destined to become a breeder parrot. She couldn't bear that thought, and besides, she'd come to like the little bugger. More interestingly, he'd come to like her, too. She would have adopted half of the animals at the shelter if her apartment complex allowed more than caged pets.

A quick Internet search revealed that Mr. Bromley was a U.S. Congressman. She returned to the drive. "Please don't let me find anything really scuzzy on here. I don't want to be known as the "whistleblower" all over CNN and the Internet." Her policy was never to read clients' files unless something screamed *sick and illegal.* Fortunately that hadn't happened yet.

She reached for her mug of coffee amidst the clutter of computer parts. The few who saw her work space were always amazed that she could function in it. She told them she had a system, which was sort of a lie. It was more like, if everything was out in the open, she'd eventually find it.

An hour later, she popped chocolate-covered cranberries into her mouth as she unearthed bits of data. "Come on, baby, oh, yes, that's it. There's the sensitive folder, but where's the presentation?"

Orn'ry always murmured when she talked to herself, which made her feel not so alone. She opened *Upcoming Issues* and found pictures and text documents with innocuous names. She double clicked on one, hands over her eyes, peeking through the cracks of her fingers. If it was something disturbing, she didn't want it seared into her subconscious.

"Yuck." Well, she now had an idea of how the laptop might have ended up in a pool. At least the woman draped over a diving board wearing nothing but high heels was way older than legal age. Amy would bet she was not the Senator's wife and had no interest in confirming her suspicion.

"Immoral maybe, but not creepy or illegal."

Her body usually started craving sleep at about three in the morning, and at four her scratchy eyes said, *Enough!* Mr. Bromley was in California, and since she was in Annapolis, Maryland, that meant she had a couple of hours in the morning to jump back on it before his meeting.

She was going to transfer Orn'ry to his cage, but he was asleep, his shoulders hunched, the feathers at the side of his face fanning his beak. She left him there and dragged herself off to bed.

She was never too tired to hope for one of her dreams, the ones that woke her in panting breaths and damp with perspiration. A man whose face was always in shadow, touching, kissing, loving her. The same man in every dream. She grinned. Even in her dreams she wasn't a slut.

She *had* seen his body, all of it, lean but muscular, olive skin, with a head full of dark, soft waves. In these dreams, she loved and was loved, there as never in her life. She was safe to let herself go. The only way he would break her heart was if she stopped dreaming about him. Four months ago, she had never felt an orgasm. Now she experienced the shattering of her body and soul every night. What an amazing realization, that she could physically experience what she dreamed about.

She slipped through the hypnagogic state of sleep, where she sometimes heard voices, and dove into REM. Deep in an ordinary dream her eyes snapped open, her heart thrashing against her ribs. She hadn't heard a thing, couldn't see a thing, but she knew someone was there.

Her second thought—after *Oh, shit, someone's in my room!*—was: *What can I use as a weapon?* Clock. Brass table lamp with sharp corners. Bingo. Her hand darted out to grab it and collided with hard flesh. Before she could scream, he was on top of her, his hand over her mouth.

"I'm not going to hurt you," he said.

Oh, God, he was going to rape her and kill her and cut her up in pieces. *This can't be happening. Fight! Kick!* But he was on top of her, his weight pinning her down. Panic squeezed her chest.

He shifted to the side, reaching for something. She heard a click. Knife? Gun?

Light flooded the room. She blinked in the sudden onslaught. Her eyes focused on the man in front of her. Gorgeous, with gray-blue eyes, and dark brown, wavy hair, he didn't look like a crazed rapist killer. That didn't ease her fear any more than his words of assurance did.

It hit her then. He made no attempt to hide his face. *That's because he doesn't intend to leave a witness.* Whimpering sounds emanated from her, as though a small animal was trapped in her chest. She quieted them, because, dammit, she wasn't going to go down like a mouse beneath an eagle's talons.

He leaned close. A gold cross on a chain dangled before her eyes. The sight of it was surreal. A cross on a killer. If he tried to kiss her she'd spit in his face or, better yet, tear off his lip with her teeth.

His mouth hovered just above her cheek. He spoke in a low, soft voice that would be soothing if he wasn't a terrifying intruder. "Amy, my name is Lucas, and there are things I need to tell you. I'm sorry, really sorry, I had to do it this way. I didn't have time to gain your trust. Am I hurting you?"

She'd swear by the concern in his eyes that he cared about her comfort. He pressed his hand over her mouth only as much as necessary. She shook her head. Her heart pounded so hard she thought it might explode.

"Good. I'm here to talk to you about your father's supposed suicide."

Her brain scrambled to process his words. Her father's suicide.

*Gunshot coming from her house!*

*Spray of blood.*

*Shallow breaths.*

*His eyes wide and fearful, pleading, Save me. Save me.*

*"Daddy, no!"*

Twenty years ago, but it felt like yesterday. She'd found him in the garage that horrible day after hearing the gunshot on her way home from school. The man who claimed he loved her killed himself where he knew she'd find him. Her sole provider made no arrangements for his five-year-old's care.

The bigger question was, why was this possible rapist and murderer talking about her father's suicide? Unless he wasn't a rapist and murderer. She must be crazy, because he didn't feel like either. That's when it her: his glow wasn't like any she'd seen before. Not one color but all of them, like static on a television.

Wait a minute. Had he said her father's *supposed* suicide?

He obviously saw her curiosity. "If I release you, you won't scream? I'd rather not continue the conversation like this."

She shook her head, and he freed her. She scrambled away from him, feeling the grooves of the headboard bite into her back when she slammed into it.

He sat back on her bed, his hands on his jean-clad thighs. The hair at his neck curled from dampness. "You don't have to be afraid of me."

She almost laughed. "A stranger breaks in, and I'm supposed to be *cool* with that?"

"Amy, we're not strangers."

The way he looked at her, with a soft smile and his gaze reaching right into her soul, corkscrewed her stomach. She pushed beyond that puzzling statement. "What do you know about my father?"

He reached over and turned on the stereo in her alarm clock. Evanescence's powerful song, "Bring Me to Life," filled the room, the tune she cued to wake her this week.

"Why'd you do that?" she asked, her words crammed together. What was he going to do that he didn't want anyone to hear?

"Just in case someone is listening."

"The walls aren't that thin."

"Listening equipment can pick up conversations from over a hundred yards away, through walls thick or thin."

"Listening equipment?"

He leaned forward and for a bizarre moment she thought he was going to kiss her. His mouth grazed the shell of her ear and whispered, "My two friends, Eric, Petra, and I discovered that someone is watching us. They call us Offspring." His breath caressed her ear. "You're one, too."

"Me?" she choked out.

"It's how I finally found you. The Offspring we know about have two common links: we lived near Ft. Meade, Maryland, during the same time period, and we each had a parent who died either by suicide or accident within a year's time." He gave her a moment to absorb, looking toward the window and the darkness beyond.

She pressed her hands to her temples, trying to make sense of it. "Someone is watching you? Me?" When he nodded, she asked, "Who?"

"We don't know. Probably some facet of government, which is why we can't go to the police."

"Do you have any…proof?"

He looked toward the window again. "Not yet. We need to find other Offspring so we can put the facts together and figure out what's going on. You're the first one we contacted." He leaned close once more. "I know you have a lot of questions, or you will once you get your mind around all this. We need to meet somewhere tomorrow where we can talk more. I can't stay here much longer, in case they're watching you. They may suspect I'd come here, which makes it dangerous for me, but I had to warn you." His expression grew dark. “You can’t tell anyone what I’ve told you.”

“Warn me about what?”

“Someone you trust is going to betray you, and someone is going to die because of that betrayal. It might be you.” She shivered at his warm breath in her ear as well as his words.

The depth of his concern baffled her. He looked at her in the way someone who had loved her for a long time might look at her. All she really had to go on was the way her father looked at her, and that was such a distant memory. And he hadn’t really loved her enough after all. Except Lucas said *supposed* suicide.

“How do you know?” she asked. “About this betrayal that’s going to happen?”

“I’ll tell you tomorrow, that and everything we know.” She saw the regret on his face when he said, “I hate that you’re involved in this. We don’t even know what *this* is yet.” He released a long breath. “Be prepared. Everything you think you know is going to change.” His body went rigid as he turned down the radio and cocked his head to listen.

“What is it?” Then she heard a soft *crack*.

He looked at her, fear in his eyes. “Trouble. Protect yourself. Tell them I just broke in and I haven’t told you anything. You’re scared to death of me.” Footsteps pounded across her living room floor. He pulled a piece of paper from his jeans pocket and curled her fingers around it. “Hide this.”

Three men dressed in black burst into her bedroom. The man in front aimed a gun at them. “Freeze!” Lucas’s hands flew up as he stepped in front of her. Despite his surrender, the man squeezed the trigger. Not a loud report but a *whoosh.* A stream of blood squirted on Lucas's collar as his hand flew up to the wound in the neck. A second man stepped into the room and walked toward Lucas, who barreled toward him with his head lowered and shoulders hunched like a bull. He knocked the guy against the doorframe; his skull hit the wood with a thud.

Next, Lucas aimed for the third man who was running toward him. They wrestled, ending up in the living room and sending her goose neck lamp crashing to the floor. Lucas was more wiry muscle than bulk, but he had rage on his side. He jammed the palm of his hand into the man's face, sending blood spurting out of his nose. Instead of running toward the open door, Lucas faced the second man, who was approaching fast despite the blood trickling down his head.

Lucas wasn't trying to escape, but to take out the men one by one. With a bullet in his neck. She sat paralyzed as he dug his elbow into the man's stomach. The one with the gun, who appeared to be the leader, made no move to help his comrades. He was waiting for something. That something became obvious when Lucas's motions slowed. He blinked several times. Wobbled. His eyes rolled back, his body slackened, and he crumpled to the floor with a painful *thump.* One man limped over as another checked Lucas's pulse and peeled back an eyelid. After a nod to the man with the gun, the two hoisted Lucas up and carried him out the door.

The leader turned toward her and started to say something, but she shouted, "You shot him!"

"He was endangering you."

It was only just sinking in, that he'd been shot, that

he was probably dead because people didn't survive bullets to the neck, did they? Or if they did they were paralyzed but mostly they died. "Who are you people?"

"FBI," he said, flashing his badge so fast she could only see that it *was* a badge. The man whose features were as stark as a mask said, "This guy's been on our radar for months now. We had to wait for him to break in before we could arrest him."

"Arrest him? *You shot him!*" she said again, her scream edging into hysterical.

"He's a serial killer who's eviscerated fourteen women with a carving knife."

"He didn't have a knife."

"That you saw." He looked into her eyes. "Did he say anything to you?"

She was supposed to pretend to be afraid of Lucas. That he'd said nothing. She shook her head.

He studied her. "Nothing at all?"

"He didn't have time. You—"

"You're lucky to be alive, ma'am," he interrupted before turning and leaving.

"Shot him," she finished with a whimper. She fell limp onto the bed, a cold fog starting from her fingers and stealing over her entire self. Orn'ry was screeching in her office but she couldn't move. Trembling followed the cold, tiny seizures sparking through her muscles.

*Offspring. Her father. Betrayal.* Lucas's urgent words careened around in her head. Then the leader's words: *serial killer. Eviscerated women. Lucky to be alive.*

Lucas was right. Someone had been outside listening, watching. Watching her. A violent tremble shook her body. On wobbly legs she walked to the window and pulled open the drapes, hoping for a glimpse of the vehicle the men had arrived in. The lights that usually illuminated the parking area were off, leaving the night in darkness. She heard the sound of a car start and pull away but never saw headlights.

"Who are you people?"

She became aware of the paper in her hand, now damp from sweat. She tucked it in her pajama waistband with shaky fingers. The most bizarre thing was how worried she was for the stranger who'd broken into her apartment and scared the hell out of her. She managed to reach for the phone and dial Uncle Cyrus.

He answered on the first ring. "Amy, what's wrong?"

"A man broke in…then these men…serial killer…they shot him!" Her teeth started chattering and she couldn't utter anything else.

"I'll be right there."

CPSIA information can be obtained at www.ICGtesting.com
Printed in the USA
LVOW08s0636280516

490348LV00007B/553/P